THE FRANKLIN EXPEDITION

Published in Canada by Engen Books, St. John's, NL.

ISBN-13: 978-1-77478-039-8

Distributed by:
Engen Books
www.engenbooks.com
submissions@engenbooks.com

First mass market paperback printing: April 2021

Cover Design: Ellen Curtis

Slipstreamers Committee:
Amanda Labonté
Ali House
AJ Ryan
Ellen Curtis
Erin Vance
Lauralana Dunne
Matthew LeDrew

THE FRANKLIN EXPEDITION

PAUL CARBERRY & JD RYOT

THE FRANKLIN EXPEDITION

CHAPTER ONE

The extensive capacity of the heat pumps did little to keep the glacial cold conditions in Terror Bay out of her bones. Cassidy Cane pulled her seal skin jacket tighter, her teeth chattering even with the combined animal fur skin lining. Her trek from Gjoa Haven across King William Island had been a thoroughly unique experience. She was still not used to the creeping cold as it engulfed the cabin of her enclosed snowmobile. Spending several days inside the houses, with the fire continually burning, did little to prepare her for this trip. While she enjoyed learning the Inuit culture from the elders and playing with the children, sharing stories of her former adventures with them. Even though she enjoyed the time with them, she couldn't wait to enter the next portal. In her brief experiences with traversing between dimensions, she quickly recognized that every portal was as extraordinary as the destination. She couldn't wait to explore another strange world. She felt goosebumps break out on her arms and anticipation of this new adventure growing in the pit of her stomach.

Blinding snowstorms and complete whiteout conditions were oddly beautiful from the comfort of her enclosure. Cassidy watched as the gale whipped snow and ice pellets in her direction, the heat in a continual feud with the forces of nature. The whistle of the wind as it swept across the desolate, snow covered region was piercing, drowning out the electric hum of the engine. Cassidy had spent three days in Gjoa Haven with the Inuit settlers. Her time there was brief. Cassidy felt a deep connection with those who had called this place home. Doctor Herbert Gamgee had sent her there under the disguise of a nurse at the Continuing Care Facility, his true purpose concealed from the entire world, including Cassidy. She still didn't know the purpose of these expeditions, but she couldn't resist the temptation of adventure. Being able to experience the harsh wilderness through the eyes of the Inuit settlers gave her a new appreciation of the importance of survival techniques. Trading small trinkets and sweets with the children made her smile. Cassidy had always been against the seal hunt, the images shown on the news were horrifying and deeply disturbing. After spending three days in Gjoa Haven, learning how critical the seal was to surviving in the artic, altered her perception of the entire situation. She glanced down at her parka, her slender frame appearing paper thin underneath the abundant furs.

Doctor Gamgee had arranged everything she required to reach the next portal. A state-of-the-art snow machine capable of navigating any terrain, the triangular tracks and wide skis made crossing the rough ice quick and comfortable. The blackened windshield kept the low winter sun out of her eyes, shielding her against snow blindness. The heat pump and warm clothes kept her from freezing. An advanced GPS navigation system displayed her route towards the portal on the high-definition monitor. Her short stature and trim build afforded her stretching room in the enclosed dome of the snowmobile. Cassidy kept going over the words of Doctor Gamgee in her head, over and over. He had given her the strangest GPS coordinates to the new portal and assured her it wasn't a mistake. She was having a difficult time trusting him.

An abrupt, unexpected, change in the weather allowed the sun to shine brilliantly against the white backdrop. Shards of sparkling specters reflected sunlight spread across the horizon. Looking out over the frozen water of Terror Bay, all she could see was the windswept snow drifting over the ice fields. The ice formed jagged, jutting walls as the old sea ice defied the newly formed ice flows. Walls of towering ice made travelling on foot nearly impossible, rendering this part of the world a natural phenomenon. Round, puffy white clouds crowded the sky, the clouds outlined with black edges.

A sharp ding signalled her arrival at the coordinates. "Well, here we are." Cassidy muttered to herself as the butterflies in her stomach fluttered their wings. Here she sat, just eighty feet above the wreckage of the HMS Terror. The failed Franklin expedition had led to the loss of all one hundred and twenty-nine sailors on board. They had lost both ships for over one hundred years in the Arctic Ocean but recently discovered them, garnering a lot of interest. Through the exploration of the HMS Terror, Doctor Gamgee discovered a portal to another dimension beneath the wreckage of the derelict ship. A twelve-foot-thick sheet of ice was the only thing separating her from the portal, or so Doctor Gamgee had told her. Herbert had been vague about what he expected Cassidy to find in this new world. All that he would tell her was that she needed to look for a magnetic anomaly, and that it was vital she brought it back to him. He had been particularly assertive about that fact. Doctor Gamgee had equipped the snowmobile with a special pod, the entire frame coated in Tungsten and durable plexiglass designed to tolerate extreme temperatures. He assured her that the pod was equipped and capable of heating the exterior shell enough to melt down through the ice, while the interior would maintain safe temperatures. Once the pod cut through the ice, it would plunge straight down into the portal. Herbert had the entire ship moved just enough for her to enter before the thick sea ice formed back over the shallow waters of Terror Bay.

All she had to do was press the red button. Her finger hovered over it, the cold plastic brushing against her skin as she struggled to force down the debilitating thoughts racing through her mind. "This is crazy, Cassidy." She tried to talk herself out of pushing the button. The analytical side of her brain warned her of all the horrid events that were possible. What if the heat gave out? She would be trapped in the midst of a sheet of thick ice, which wouldn't thaw until spring in two months. What if she broke through the ice but didn't sink? She would find herself held firmly against the ice with no way back up. What if she couldn't find the portal? She would suffocate from lack of oxygen, powerless to reach the surface. What if the glass broke? She would drown while she froze to death, her muscles unable to function. A white blur rushed across Cassidy's vision, squinting against the bright sunlight, the form slowly began to take shape. A polar fox cub was scampering across the tundra. She was so hypnotized by the elegance of the young Arctic fox that she lost all track of time. She watched it play in the snow, pouncing after a few stray birds but never able to capture one in its tiny paws. Every so often she would lose sight of the critter as it retreated behind a snow drift or behind a jagged formation of ice. Eventually, the fox vanished from her line of sight for good, the animal disappearing into the winter wonderland, its white fur the perfect camouflage for the Arctic conditions.

Cassidy impulsively pushed the button as her irrational side demanded jurisdiction over her once again. Her whole body tensed, not understanding what to expect next, Cassidy held her breath and closed her eyes. She waited for something, anything, to happen. Anticipation escalated, any moment she expected to plummet on a wild descent through the thick sea ice. A wave of heat washed over her, perspiration began to form on her brow. Cautiously opening her eyes, Cassidy was disappointed to find she was sinking through the ice at a snail's pace. The frozen salt water was inching up the windshield, inch by inch the pod was melting the old ice. With her seal skin mittens, she wiped away the dripping perspiration. Cassidy contemplated removing her outer layer as the temperature continued to rise in her pod. Now she wondered if Herbert had made a miscalculation, the enclosure was starting to resemble an oven. Quickly examining the control panel, Cassidy wondered if there was a way to abort the descent. Panic was settling in, a surge of adrenaline flooding her entire system magnified the situation. She realized that no one except Doctor Gamgee knew where she was, and she wasn't sure he would come looking for her. Her breath was laboured, claustrophobia was taking over as the ice completely filled her vision. The melting sea ice turned pure white, bubbled and churned as the pod drifted downwards faster now. The sea water collected above her head, turning back into sheets of ice almost instantly.

An abrupt deviation in pressure jolted Cassidy in her seat, the pod bursting through the last layer of ice without warning. The thick glass slammed hard against the ice once before the hum of the engine returned, bright white lights illuminated the darkened waters all around her. A barren sea opened up before her, void of any marine life, mimicking the world above. Light from her pod only stretched a few feet in front of her, the darkness swallowing everything beyond its reach whole. It took several moments for her eyes to adjust, the underwater world reluctant to reveal itself to her. Cassidy had no sense of direction, she couldn't tell if she was drifting with the current or descending. Everything looked the same to her down here. After several tense moments, Cassidy spotted something swimming near the edge of her vision. She recognized the silver back and pinkish-red belly of the Arctic Char, she had seen several during her stay in Gjoa Haven, in the dining halls. In an instant, the underwater world exploded with life, drawn in by the light. A school of fish swam in all directions around the pod, dancing back and forth in her field of vision.

The blurry haze of a sunken ship started to come into

focus. The wooden frame of the ship was, remarkably still in excellent shape. Seaweed covered the entire ship, the ocean current causing it to sway back and forth in an unending dance. A towering smokestack was still intact, the long pipe listing only slightly to the left as the ship rested upright along the ocean floor. They had removed the three masts during the winter when the ship got stuck in the ice. It was a preventative measure to stop the buildup of ice on the sails and masts from capsizing the ship. They never replaced the masts; the crew was forced to abandon the HMS Terror in the ice during its third winter. The Terror, once thought destroyed by the ice flows, was intact and showed little signs of any damage. Cassidy watched in astonishment as the British Naval ship seemed to stretch endlessly into the darkness.

Suction tugged at the pod, yanking the drifting vessel downwards towards a swirling pit of darkness alongside the HMS Terror. Cassidy's vision began to blur as the pod spun out of control, a gushing roar of water grew louder, the expanding force pinning her into the seat. Her knuckles whitened as she gripped the steering wheel in a frivolous attempt to control the spiraling motion. Cassidy closed her eyes tight, waiting for the nauseous sensation to pass.

CHAPTER TWO

Cassidy felt her mind racing, powerless to tell if the visions she experienced were filtering in through her eyes or if they were embedded directly onto her brain from the portal. Every trip through the portal had a distinct effect on her, and this dimension was toying with her mind. Unable to determine if she was in a feverish dream or trapped in another reality, Cassidy waited for the feeling to pass. A crisp breeze sent shudders throughout her entire body, her knees trembled, and goosebumps sprang out all over her body. She crossed her arms over her chest, rubbing her upper body to generate warmth.

Visions of the past, present and future blended together. The overload of information caused her brain to pound, every detail flickered in her head just long enough to register. She couldn't concentrate long enough to comprehend any meaning, the torrent of memories flooding over her like a waterfall. Images of old British-style ships sailing through rough waves laden with large pans of ice were dominant over all other pictures being painted in her head.

"What are you doing here?" A man's voice reverberated in Cassidy's cranium. She glanced around in all directions, but all she could see was blackness. She closed her eyes and the impressions of the ships and frozen world returned to her.

"Where are you?" Cassidy questioned. She had encountered nothing like this in the other portals. Was this dimension entirely in her mind, or was she now only realizing that fact?

"That is not relevant right now." His commanding voice was void emotion. "What is critical is that you comprehend why you are here."

"What do you mean?" A pair of ships trapped in the ice came into focus, a line of sailors walking away from the ships stretched far. The men were pulling sleds, overwhelmed with supplies as they trudged across the ice.

"Do you know why you have come to this wretched place?" Somehow, Cassidy knew the voice belonged to one man on the ice.

"I don't even know what this place is?" Curiosity and intrigue captured all of her attention, drawing her focus towards every detail she could discover. The men's faces were veiled from view, everybody had their faces shrouded in scarves. Their outer winter slops were frozen stiff and covered in filth.

"Creation of this dimension was born of heroic tragedy, the lost souls here doomed to live out their lives defending a tragic secret. The origin of their suffering is also the source of your salvation." A man on the ice stalled, lifting his head up towards Cassidy. She felt his eyes upon her, an ice-cold sensation coursed through her veins.

"Salvation of my planet?" Cassidy studied the man's

face, his clean-shaven face riddled with ice burns. Time aged his eyes far beyond the man's years, his brown eyes saturated with immeasurable misery.

The man now stood alone of the open ice, the silhouette of the two ships prominent in the background. "Not just salvation for your planet. Rather, it can be the redemption for all mankind, in the proper hands." As he spoke, Cassidy noticed his yellow teeth and bloodied gums.

Cassidy opened her eyes and was startled to discover herself surrounded by the sailors she had seen on the ice. They trudged past her on both sides, neither man glancing up from their desolate journey to pay her any attention. "I don't understand. Who are you?"

"I was once someone to you, now I am no one of any importance. My great discovery led to my terrible fate and the damnation of my crew." Underneath his thick, wool jacket Cassidy noticed golden buttons on his dress uniform. She recognized the style of his garments, once dawned by the British Royal Navy. He stood tall and proud, a stoic figure underneath the many layers of clothes protecting him from the extreme cold. "My pride would not allow me to let go of our extraordinary discovery. It remained until the bitter end, and now we are here waiting for liberation."

"I still don't understand," Cassidy called out, the swarm of sailors pushing her away from him. They carried her away from him without saying a word. She struggled against them, never able to elude their grasp even though she couldn't feel them touching her. "I can help you." Cassidy felt a blast of frosty cold air and a blizzard of snow clouded her vision. She covered her eyes with her hand, squinting against the golden light that loomed over her. The silvery glow grew outwards, an explosion of pure white forced her to clench her eyelids shut. When she opened them again, she found herself in an officer's berth aboard a ship. The bed was narrow and short, even for her. Drawers underneath utilized every inch of space. The sheets were neatly folded, the thin pillow placed neatly at the head of the bed. A tiny nightstand next to the bed had a drained glass and a bottle of black rum, the residue of the black liquid remained from the finished drink.

A tiny window faced out over an infinite ocean; the white-capped waves rolled into the horizon in a perpetual ripple. Cassidy turned around and narrowly avoided bumping her head against the low door frame. She stepped into the corridor, careening into the wall as her legs still adjusted to the swell of the ocean. "Hello," Cassidy called out, her voice echoing back to her. It was eerily silent aboard this ship. The melodies of crashing waves were distant, as if she was far removed from the middle of the ocean. The hallway was lavishly carpeted, the red and blue colours resembled the union jack. At the end of the hallway was a solid oak door, the brass knob polished to a glorious luster. Swaying back and forth with the cadence of the ship, Cassidy made her way towards the exit. Something was calling her towards it, drawing her in.

On the wall next to the door, an oil painting hung prominently on display. She paused to admire the painted image. A British Officer in his dress uniform. Golden shoulder boards accented his black tunic, buttons resembling gold coins ran in pairs down the center of his double-breasted jacket. Medals and crosses affixed to his chest spoke of courageous deeds and boundless loyalty to duty. A stiff white collar covered most of his neck, reaching to his chin. Vibrant, hazel-brown eyes looked proudly into the future with a smug sense of accomplishment and self-worth. Cassidy couldn't help but crack a smile at the man's hair, it didn't suit the stature of the portrait. Hair stuck off the sides of his head in curly lumps, the top of his head bald. Her lips curled into a gentle grin, a faint chuckle escaped her throat. Her soft laughter seemed to disappear into thin air, the echo that should have existed was replaced by silence. The door at the end of the hallway began to demand Cassidy's focus. Somehow, she knew that where the echo had vanished. She ran her fingers over the solid oak door, she felt an immense power emanating from the other side. Now she understood that this was a dream, and once she walked through this door, she would appear in its awaiting dimension.

Again, her heart raced in her chest as her rational side tried to reason with the situation she was facing. Her growing concern was the fear of coming out of the other side of this portal underneath the frozen ocean. Reaching out for the brass handle, Cassidy clenched her muscular frame in anticipation, not knowing what awaited her on the other side. With her eyes shut, she yanked the door open and felt herself falling.

CHAPTER THREE

Cassidy had her eyes clamped shut, but she recognized she was on a ship. She felt the wooden boards of the weathered decking. Underneath her, the swell of the waves shook the ship back and forth. Roaring waves crashed back into the ocean as a mighty wind filled the sails of the ships, the canvas fluttering above her. A strong scent of brine filled her nostrils. The sun was bright, the warm rays beating against her skin and negated the biting sting of the wintery winds. Below her hands, the boards were waterlogged and slick from the melting frost. She leaned backward on her knees, stretching out her abdominal muscles.

"You there, how d'you find yourself on my ship?" A deep, booming voice startled Cassidy. "Answer me or find yourself overboard." She noted a thick, British accent coated his speech.

Opening her eyes, the gleaming white light of the sun shrouded her vision. She shielded her eyes with the back of her hand, the looming shadow of a tall man slowly taking shape in front of her. "Where am I?" Her voice was flat and feeble, the side effects of travelling through the portal still had control over her.

"Do not dodge my questions with those of your own. I demand an explanation as to why a youthful lady would stow away on the Lord Commander's ship?" The luster of the sun began to fail, slowly revealing the features of the man standing before Cassidy. A sense of déjà vu washed over her, as if she had met this man somewhere before as she peered into his hazel eyes. A triangular brimmed hat propped on his head; locks of white hair coiled into tight, eccentric circles flowed out from underneath. "I grow impatient."

"I can't provide an answer to that." Too drained from traversing the portal, Cassidy couldn't even come up with a false excuse. With tremendous exertion, she forced her exhausted legs to stand. Every muscle fiber twitched and knotted. Painful daggers pierced at her body from within.

"Count yourself lucky that I have neither the time nor the heart to punish you." The man snapped his fingers, stomping footsteps pounded against the decking as two sailors approached. "Whatever your reasons, they are of little concern. Where we are heading is punishment enough." A frosty burst of sea water showered over the deck, the droplets of water beading on her seal skin parka. Something caught the interest of the captain, his stare fixed on a point far behind her. Cassidy turned her gaze to join the commander. It was as if the ocean had frozen instantly, the white caps curling upward toward the splendid rays of sunshine. A howling wind cut across the snow, hiding the source of the captain's amazement. Nestled into the horizon, a white castle, sprouting from the ice like a dazzling crystal, towered high above them. Low, growling roars carried in the wind from the prodigious structure.

"You summoned us, Sir Franklin." An inexperienced, nervous voice broke Cassidy's concentration.

Two young sailors, dressed identically, stood at attention in front of the captain. Their wool knit hats pulled down to their eyebrows. Both men wore heavy, cotton tunics that had become frozen stiff from the salty mist. "Young lad, Francis, if I'm not mistaken."

The taller of the two seamen stepped forward, bowing his head. "Yes, sir." His feeble voice squeaked, the poor young man still progressing through adolescence. His face still riddled with acne and scars.

"Very good then. Take…" Sir Franklin's face flushed with embarrassment, turning his checks a bright red. "Excuse me, young lady, I've not behaved like an honorable gentleman. Please forgive me but I am Sir Jack Franklin, Commander of the HMS Fear," he held out his hand. "And who do I have the pleasure?"

Cassidy tried to shake his hand, but he took her hand in his, and bowed down to kiss it. Before she understood what was happening, he tipped his hat to her. "Cassidy Cane," she responded sharply, outraged by his abrupt action, drawing her hand backward.

"Well, Francis, please escort Miss Cane below deck and make sure they feed her," Sir Franklin turned his attention away from Cassidy. "And you, young man, tell Sir Irving that we will make our way to the shore. Make sure that a crew informs the Erebus of our intentions. I shall accompany the party to explore this castle. Maybe this is where my father landed."

"Aye, aye, Sir." The young lad clicked his heels together and carried on about his duties.

Young Francis grabbed Cassidy's arm, but she defiantly yanked it away. "I will accompany you." She was not about to be left on board this strange ship.

Shock furled Sir Franklin's brow, he was not a man who accepted defiance. "Miss Cane…"

"Call me Cassidy, and this is not up for deliberation." she asserted herself.

"This is my ship," Jack raised his voice.

"I am not one of your sailors," Cassidy cut him off. "They will not treat me as such."

The wind was silenced like a scolded dog. Cassidy stood in defiance of the Captain, the tension between them rising swiftly. Young Francis bowed his head down to look at his boots, not wanting to make eye contact with his Captain. For what seemed like an eternity, Sir Franklin pondered his next words. "Have it your way then. It makes no difference to us."

"Sir, what would you have me do now?" Francis asked.

"Go help the men gather provisions for the night," Sir Franklin barked without hesitation. The young sailor scurried off to join the commotion rising from behind them.

Cassidy stepped forward. "What would you like me to do?"

"You are not one of my sailors." Sir Franklin tried his best to sound cordial, but his finest effort did little hide his indignation. "I will simply propose that you remain out of trouble. I do not have the men to spare looking after you."

Cassidy felt insulted. Cassidy was more than capable of taking care of herself, and she was positive the men aboard the HMS Fear could learn a thing or two from her. "You don't have to worry about me." She spit out each word, the sting of the insult still fresh.

"There you are Sir Franklin." An exceptionally tall man snuck up behind them, not sensing the tension between them. He was clad in the same clothes as Jack but looked different from his counterpart. His jacket wasn't stiff, but dangled loosely from his broad shoulders, the fabric dancing in the breeze. His cheeks were rosy and an extreme contrast to his pale blue eyes. "I need to speak to you."

"What is it, mister Irving?" Sir Franklin sounded annoyed by the younger man.

"If it pleases you, a private counsel may be beneficial." Irving spoke gently. His wig, while comparable to Sir Franklin's, appeared to be of poorer quality. The white curls hung loosely just above his shoulders with messy, stray hairs going in all directions.

"I don't have time for that," Sir Franklin rolled his eyes at the proposition. "Just get on with it man."

"Well Sir, there appears to be a problem with the compass. The dial just spins around in random directions." Irving presented the facts.

"Gibberish, that compass is brand new." Sir Franklin shook his head. "It employs the latest technology available, just like every other piece of equipment under my command. I guarantee you it is not a malfunction of the equipment."

"With all due respect Sir, it operates based on its capacity to detect magnetic fields. There is no human error possible because it's purely mechanical." Irving spoke calmly and ignored the Captain's irritation. He reached into his pocket, retrieving a pack of cigarettes and matches. He shielded the smoke and struck a match in his hand with practiced expertise, drawing in a slow puff. "I can give a rough bearing to Sir Coizer on the Erebus, but I'm not able to provide him the exact location. I recommend that we wait here for him. They are not that far behind us, anyway."

"I will take it under advisement. In the meantime, Sir Irving, I suggest that you try to fix that compass of yours." Sir Franklin turned his nose at the acrid odor of cigarette smoke. The breeze blew it right into his face.

"He will not be able to fix it." Cassidy interjected.

"What do you know of it?" Sir Franklin chuckled. "I have serious doubts you are privy to the knowledge of this invention." He shot Irving a sly grin which the other officer did not reciprocate.

Not wishing to expose her identity, revealing the fact that she was an inter-dimensional traveller, choosing her words carefully. "I know just as much as any member of your crew. I've seen this happen before."

"Seen this happen before?" Sir Franklin didn't wait for an answer. "This is the first time we have used the invention aboard any vessel."

Cassidy felt her heart racing, both men gawking at her quizzically. She had vaulted into the midst of an argument she had no benefit of winning. All she had to do was keep her opinion to herself, and she would have discovered the magnetic anomaly, anyway. "This new technology isn't much more advanced than putting a leaf in a puddle of water." Both men remained still, a bewildered look plastered on their faces.

"I've never heard of that method being employed except by the unsophisticated savages." Sir Franklin scoffed. "Hardly reliable and inconsequential to our situation here."

She may have fooled Sir Franklin, but Irving's gaze remained glued on her. Cassidy felt warm, she could feel the perspiration beading on her goose bumped flesh. "I'm just trying to say that people used to believe that it worked." Cassidy knew the truth, she had stumbled upon her destination without having invested in any effort. By saying anything, all she did was put her chance of discovering the artifact at risk. Irving continued to study her with untrusting eyes. "Now we have a new compass that we believe works without fail."

"Sir Irving, please send a message to the Erebus immediately. I do not want to delay any further than what is necessary." Sir Franklin brushed off Irving by waving his hand theatrically. "Now, Miss Cane, will you escort me to the mess hall for a glass of whisky?" Irving left quietly, keeping the line of sight between them until he vanished through one of the doors.

Cassidy turned her back to Sir Franklin, admiring the natural beauty of the tundra. Looking closer at the white castle, she could see the weathered grey stones underneath. "I don't drink whisky."

"Well, I could offer you some of my personal black rum." Sir Franklin softened the tone of his voice. "The others will be envious."

"Did you say black rum?" That triggered Cassidy's subconscious. She recalled seeing a bottle of black rum on the nightstand in the officer's berth. That feverish dream must have meant something. It had to be connected to this world somehow. Was this all part of some puzzle she would have to piece together to discover the artifact Doctor Gamgee required from this realm?

"Very well then, I will fetch my steward and have him prepare us two drinks before we depart." Sir Franklin turned to leave. "If it pleases you, we could take our drink here on deck."

"That will do just fine, Sir." Cassidy replied graciously, relishing in the opportunity to collect her thoughts alone. The captain's footprints could be heard echoing into the cold air. Four giant towers had been erected into each corner of the castle; each pillar was a near perfect circle. Each tower had windows sporadically placed throughout the structure, with a canopy covering each landing from the elements. The stairs at the front of the building had been drawn out as far as they could, each step about four feet wide. Broken off the hinges, one side of the double wooden door lay battered against ground. The iron frame twisted and distorted from some horrific struggle years ago. Layer upon layer of ice had built up over the stones from previous winters. The ice was so white it looked blue in the shadows. It appeared to be vacant, there were no signs of activity outside in the snow-covered courtyard.

"Your drink, my lady."

Cassidy could feel the warm breath on her neck. She spun around immediately, coming face to face with a scruffy-looking sailor. Long strands of black, greasy hair clung to his face. His breath reeked of salt fish and whisky. He held out a glass half-filled with the black rum Sir Franklin had offered.

"Thank you." Cassidy took possession of the glass, wondering if it was the same one from her vision. The sailor brushed back a stray clump of greasy hair, grinned a toothless smile and took his leave without uttering another word. She placed the drink on the rail, looking back out over the ice-packed waters separating the HMS Fear from solid ice. The water was virtually black, making the ice stand out even more against the backdrop.

How deep was this water?

Footsteps approached the rail, the clank of Sir Franklin's glass against the rail startled her. He didn't say a word, he just leaned against the rail and glanced out over the water. "I've been chasing after my father for years. So many I've actually lost count now." He raised his glass. "To Sir John Franklin." They clinked their glasses together. Cassidy wondered what the failed Franklin expedition had to do with this realm. The further she dug into this mystery, the deeper the layers went. Somehow, earth's dimension was directly connected to this realm. Events that took place aboard the HMS Terror and HMS Erebus had shaped the structure of this alternate world.

Or was it the other way around?

The black rum burned all the way down, the liquid splashing into her empty stomach. She coughed, holding her forearm up to her face to stifle the sound. "That's strong."

Sir Franklin nodded his head. "It's from my private

cache." He tilted his glass towards the water, letting a drop tumble out of the glass and join the dark water below. "Straight from the casks of the gods they say." He bowed his head towards the water and raised his glass to an imaginary figure. "I used to believe that the gods watch over us." His voice was bitter, filled with a deep hatred that Cassidy could feel. "Until the first time I lost a man at sea. These dark waters contain demons that reach up from below the shadowy depths and drag us down in the cold grave." He turned towards her, placed his hand on her shoulder and stared directly into her eyes. "The sea will always win. It takes our loved ones, our friends and the people we work with. It will take everything from those who try to defy it. These waters are so black because of the souls it has devoured."

Cassidy took another sip of her black rum, this time the burn didn't last as long. The dark liquid caused a warm tingle to radiate throughout her body. The words of Sir Franklin were heavy with regret, a deep pain coursed through his veins. Water and ice were not the normal area of study for Cassidy. It was at this moment that she realized she missed being an archaeologist, she missed being a teacher. She finished the last of her drink, slamming the glass down on the rail in triumph. "Thank you for the rum." Cassidy was determined she wouldn't let these darkened waters consume her.

"Thank you for listening to this old man ramble." Sir Franklin finished off his own drink, taking both glasses as he turned to leave. "Follow me to the mess. The rations for our meal have been prepared. Once we finish eating everything else should be ready."

Now that she had discovered her sea legs, Cassidy could navigate the slick deck with ease. She could keep pace with the veteran sailor, she walked into the galley with him. The tight entrance was deceiving, the room expanded into a much larger space than she would have thought possible. Furnished with lavish art, high-end furniture and a giant dining room table, Cassidy assumed that she was in the officer's mess hall. A rush of hot air surrounded her; the room was being heated somehow. She hung up her hat on a coat rack nestled in the room's corner and took off her jacket. Every eye in the room gave her a quick stare, her clothing must have seemed odd to the crew of the ship. She wore a beaver skin vest over a loose-fitting white blouse, her feminine figure expertly hidden from the gawking men.

A chair was pulled out for her, young Francis held the chair for her with a curt smile on his face. After being in this new dimension for a short time, she realized that the sailors were trying to be gentlemen. She tried not to take offence to their gestures, but she didn't appreciate being treated this way. If the men aboard this ship knew all the things she had accomplished in the last few weeks since exploring the dimensions, they would look at her differently. She sat down in the sturdy wooden chair, the blue cushion surprisingly soft. The dining table was long enough to seat eight people on either side, the darkened mahogany wood was showing the signs of being at sea for too long. Cassidy found herself to the left of Sir Franklin, she sat with her back to the wall. She could watch as all the officers filed into the room. The men shared small talk as they went about their business of hanging up their winter slops.

Servers wearing white jackets and chef's hats brought out plates filled with steaming hot food. Having prepared it below deck, the stewards entered the room from a set of stairs off to the left. Cassidy knew that the officers tried their best to hide the higher quality of food from their sailors. Jealousy and envy could cause a mutiny, even though everyone knew that the officers ate better. Mounds of creamed potatoes, carrots and peas smothered in gravy made her mouth water. The pork roast beneath it all looked succulent. "Thank you," Cassidy said as a steward placed a plate in front of her. After only a few minutes, everyone sat down at the table had their dinner in front of them. The waiters brought out fresh baked buns with butter, and they had placed bottles of red wine and whisky on the table.

"Father, Praise You for friendship and family.

Thank You for bringing us together today to share a meal. The people in our lives bring us such joy, and we are grateful for time spent in fellowship together.

Help us use this time to bond closer as a group and learn to love each other more.

Bless our appetites, both physical and spiritual, to honor You in all we do. In Jesus' Name, Amen."

Sir Franklin said grace, the other men at the table all bowed their heads. He spoke with conviction but with a subtle softness required of a clergyman. The words he spoke flowed graciously off his tongue. Practiced time and time again, he didn't stutter once. The sound of cutlery clanging off the plates rang out throughout the dining hall. Most of the men didn't even bother to look up except to accept a glass of wine. Cassidy met eyes with Irving. He was leaning towards a shorter, older man. They were definitely talking about her; Cassidy could see Irving pointing at her with his fork as he spoke. She leaned towards Sir Franklin. "Who is that man Irving is speaking with?"

Sir Franklin finished chewing his food, washing it all down with a large gulp of red wine. "That is ice master Peglar."

"What does an ice master do?" Cassidy asked curiously.

"They are precious members of any ship sailing through the arctic waters." Sir Franklin said. "They are experts in navigation, fishing, hunting and survival on the ice. He will accompany us to the castle."

Quickly looking around the table, Cassidy couldn't help but wonder who else would join them. "Are we leaving soon?"

"We will be headed out onto the ice as soon as possible." Sir Franklin responded quickly, abruptly turning his attention away from Cassidy. She sat there, listening to the different conversations taking place around the table. The atmosphere was buzzing with rumors and gossip. Everyone had their opinion about what they would find in the castle. Some men thought it would be empty, others believed it would be haunted, while some people thought an ice princess lived there. Cassidy did her best to listen in on the conversation that Irving and Peglar were having, but they must have realized she noticed that they were talking about her. Both men had remained huddled close together, their voices hardly rising above a whisper. Anticipation started to build; the thrill of adventure was edging closer. Sir Franklin rose and the rest of the men stopped eating, rising to join their captain. "Well, let us head to the skiff, we want to make sure we get to the castle before sunset."

CHAPTER FOUR

The boat's gunwales dropped inch by inch, each jostling descent interrupted by an abrupt halt. Groans and grunts from the men lowering the ship grew louder with each passing moment. Strain forced the rope to dig into the sailor's hands, with each drop the boat sank further down before they caught the ropes. Cassidy bounced around on the hard wooden platform that served as her seat. Once they reached the water, the sailors used their ores to navigate towards the coast. Men with large spikes pushed away loose fragments of ice that threatened to damage the hull. The water was as black as oil, the pure darkness threatening to engulf anyone foolish enough to enter. The waves rocked the much smaller whaling boat, the sheer force of the ocean on full display. With every surge that raised the boat, a nauseous sensation would rise in her stomach. Fear would drive that feeling aside as they crashed back down into the ice-cold water.

None of the men showed any fear. They all went about their business, not paying any attention to the strong waves beneath them. Cassidy was glad that she didn't have any assigned duties. She didn't have her sea legs and years of being an archeologist made her miss standing barefoot, with the earth beneath her feet. Sir Franklin stood in the center of the whaling ship, expertly directing his crew as they performed their services. She watched Peglar and Irving as they concentrated on the shore, concocting a strategy to reach the shore. Ice had built up against the rugged coast, the silvery wall towering seven feet above them in some places. The other unnamed members of the crew worked faithfully to paddle and maneuver the boat to the shore. Sailors struggled with the effort, beads of perspiration dripped down their foreheads as they toiled relentlessly. Overheated by their heavy outer layers, some men removed their coats despite the stinging cold chill rising from the water.

"Mr. Peglar, what is our best option here?" Sir Franklin's voice lifted above the anguished cries of the struggling sailors.

"Sir, just order the men to bring us alongside the shore," Peglar pointed straight ahead. "Mr. Irving and I will take care of the rest."

"You heard the ice master, men," Sir Franklin shouted passionately. "Not much further now."

The tired sailors moaned a half-hearted hurrah, before returning to their duties. It was a tedious, strenuous process as the men paddled towards the coast. They had to slow down every time a sizable block of ice threatened to damage the boat. High waves lifted the colossal sized shards of ice dangerously close to the edge of the boat. If just one of those miniature icebergs landed in the ship, they would capsize in an instant. One man jabbed at a hunk of ice, the sharp edge of his pike dug in deep. He tried to yank the head out, but it lodged in tight. A wave raised the schooner up as the iceberg fell down on the other side, nearly ripping the poor, young sailor clear out of the boat. Cassidy leapt forward, catching him around the waist just before he tumbled out of the boat. Embarrassment swept over his face as the pike jerked out of his hand, slipping into the blackened waters.

Everyone aboard stared at the young man, snickering laughter erupted from the other men as they attended to their business. Cassidy knew they directed the laughter towards the unfortunate sailor who nearly fell overboard and had been saved by a woman. Still holding her arms around his stomach, Cassidy released him from her grip. He spun and acknowledged his gratitude towards her, having earned his respect. A shadow crept over the boat, the towering wall of ice loomed ominously above them. A sudden chill gripped her, the sun fading behind the elevated ice wall.

Knelt down at the edge of the boat, Irving and Peglar dug through a bag stuffed with various tools. Peglar retrieved an axe, the dull blade full of indentations and scrapes. "Maintain the boat as steady as possible now boys." Carefully lifting the axe above his head, Peglar starting hacking away at the ice wall. Broken fragments of ice scattered across the deck and back into the sea. The sailors held the ship as steady as they could, but the bobbing water made it challenging to strike the same place. Once the hole was deep enough, Peglar planted one foot into the ice and used it to steady himself. As the waves caused the boat underneath him to shift, the ice master bent his knee in cadence with the rolling waves. Peglar continued to hack away at the ice with the dulled blade, chiseling out a set of steps into the bank. "There, that ought to do it," He proclaimed through laboured breathing. He ascended the makeshift stairs and peered down at them.

"Do you see anything?" Irving called out, gesturing for the others to remain aboard the whaling boat.

With his back turned, Peglar disappeared from view temporarily. His footsteps crunching in the crust as he moved around. "Nothing of any danger, Sir." His voice sounded remote, the wind carrying it away from them.

"After you, gentlemen." Sir Franklin ushered the sailors up the ice stairs. One by one, the men dashed up the stairs. Cassidy took notice of the silver spikes at the bottom of the men's boots, the grips digging into the glistening surface. Irving, Sir Franklin and Cassidy were the only people remaining in the boat. They tossed lengths of rope back down into the ship, Irving tied knots into the handles of the bags carrying the party's provisions. Steadily, the sailors hoisted the supplies. The rope fell back down into the waiting arms of Irving, who secured the ends to a five-foot-long toboggan.

"After you, Miss Cane." Irving offered Cassidy his hand as they hauled the toboggan up over the ridge.

Cassidy placed her boot into the foothold, discovering it troublesome to find her footing. Frigid cold sensations ran up her arm as she placed her hand in the gaps. Something deep inside the ice seemed to percolate out of the carved holes. A cold unlike anything she had ever experienced washed over her, draining the warmth from her very essence. Her hands struggled to grasp a firm grip, but she didn't want to show any shortcoming in front of the sailors. Cassidy worried, her feet slipping out from underneath her, she scampered up the makeshift stairs hurriedly. As if anticipating her endeavors, the youthful sailor she had saved earlier, graciously held out his hand for her, hauling her up onto the shore. "Are you all right?" The young man asked.

Cassidy brushed the sleet off her pants. "Yes, I am, thank you." His pale blue eyes were so light, they appeared to be grey. A thin moustache rested on his lip like a black rim left behind from a glass. She stood up under her own power, finding herself uncomfortably close to the young man. "What is your name again?" Not remembering if she had ever known it.

With a tilt of his hat, the young man revealed a scruffy mop of curly black hair. "My name is Tommy Seeley."

"Ordinary seaman Seeley." Irving's head poked above the ice. "Stop lolly-gagging around and help Sir Franklin up." Irving pulled himself up and joined Cassidy. Tommy rushed over to help the Captain over the ledge, Sir Franklin was out of breath from the effort. "Well don't just stand there, gentlemen, these supplies need to be loaded aboard the skiff and brough to the castle. Seeley and Edwards, scout ahead and make sure we aren't walking into any trouble." Irving barked orders at his men. "We don't want any surprises when we get to the castle now."

"Yes sir." A harmony of voices responded in unison. Everyone scurrying about their business without hesitation. Years of obedience drilled into them, encouraging them forward as a company.

A large, long ranging mountain chain appeared behind the castle. Cassidy had not noticed them from the ship, but the jagged formation reached far into the sky not too far from where the castle nestled. She thought it would be the perfect location to defend, the mountains and shorelines offering great protection from all angles. Giant formations of ice and snow blended into the horizon, merging into the clouds above. Loud scraping caught her attention, the men had loaded the toboggan with all the supplies and were hauling it towards the castle. She could see Tommy far ahead with Edwards, their bodies blurring into two black specks as they scouted ahead. A low melody started to rise from the sailors as they worked in unison to pull the skiff across the crusted surface.

"Stay close to us. If the wind picks up, we could all get separated if we are too far apart." Peglar startled Cassidy. His speech was low and throaty, it was the first real time she had heard him speak directly to her. "I've seen people get twisted around in a matter of minutes. Stumbled across the frozen carcasses of my friends I had been walking alongside." Wisdom and experience weathered Peglar's soulful, emerald eyes. There was a deep sadness saturating the iris of his eyes, his black pupils mirroring the ocean water. Cassidy nodded her head, acknowledging his warning. She made sure she kept pace with Peglar, who was leading the two officers, making certain she remained in the midst of the pack. She had been trapped in a sandstorm before, the dynamic force of mother nature wasn't something to oppose. Sandstorms could materialize out of thin air and without warning, not unlike the fickle weather of this frozen wasteland.

"How long do you think it will take to uncover any evidence in there?" Irving asked Sir Franklin, his voice distorted by the approaching wind.

"If my father is here, we will know immediately." Sir Franklin's voice carried more heavily on the wind. "He wouldn't have any reason to hide from us. He would recognize our sails."

They followed in the tracks left behind by the skiff. The trail already beaten down. Without warning, the wind's intensity increased and whirled the snow around in blinding swirls. Cassidy lost track of the men pulling the sled within seconds. She had to squint against the pelting snow, the ice pellets hurt her eyes as the wind whipped a torrent of tiny daggers into her face. She closed her eyes for a second to protect them, when the gale passed, she opened her eyes again. Barren, white tundra stretched out for as far as she could see. "Hello?" Cassidy yelled out nervously against the white-out conditions. The tracks were gone. "I'm over here." She took a moment to compose herself and tried to remember her training. After taking a moment to survey the ground around her feet, she realized that she stumbled just a few feet from the tracks. She tucked her head into her chest, bracing herself against the barrage of snow pellets.

"Stay close, Miss Cane." Peglar reached out from the blanketing wall of snow, escorting her towards the rest of the party. "Until this storm passes, wear these." The ice master handed her a pair of wire-framed goggles. Placing them over her head, she found the straps dug into the sides of her skull. Able to see without squinting against the wind, she kept pace with the sailors as they trudged across the tundra. After several minutes, they arrived at the staircase of the castle.

A loud creaking noise groaned out as Irving opened the door, the metal hinges screeching high pitched wails. Cassidy followed closely behind Sir Franklin, accompanying him up the stairs. The faint flicker of torch light danced down the stone passageway. They followed the source of the light; The hallway protected them against the wind and pelting snow. They rounded the corner and felt the scorching heat from a torch, left behind in a holder hung on the wall. The corridor opened into a grand chamber. Irving gathered all the sailors around the giant hearth, fumbling with matches and logs trying to light a fire. They had already lit several of the torches placed around the corridor, the shifting light casting their silhouettes across the hall.

A roaring boom engulfed the room as a giant flame illuminated the murkiest corners of the great hall. The once smooth stones, now distorted by harsh weather, pitted and scarred them over the years. Beneath the whistle of the wind that ripped through the open window, Cassidy heard a melody of birds chirping in the rafters. Trees sprouted up from the earth, roots reached out across the fractured stone floor. Grime covered the once brilliant red tablecloths. Ancient wooden tables and chairs scattered across the room by the wind, long abandoned by the former inhabitants. Whispers of the past echoed from the walls. They recounted tales of past hardships, lives lost and of agony suffered out here on this desolate strip of earth. A wave of warmth from the fire fought against the savage chill, the warmth unable to stall the seeping coldness from the windows. The sailors huddled near the roaring blaze in the hearth, Sir Franklin joined them. Cassidy huddled into the circle; everybody did their best to shake the coldness out of their bones.

"It appears the castle has been long deserted, Sir." Irving broke the silence first.

Disappointment and resentment lingered on Sir Franklin's expression. "It would appear so," He replied wistfully. "But we have the whole night to explore and gather any evidence there may be." With a twist, he shifted towards his company and positioned himself at the center of their huddle. "Sir Irving, have the men set up the stoves. We shall clean off the tables here and eat near the warmth of the fire. We will also need to set up a place to rest for the night. Have two of your men scout out a suitable location."

"Aye, Sir," Irving replied. "Seeley and Edwards, take one shotgun with you. Have a look around and after lunch we shall set up camp for the night. The rest of you prepare the stoves and rations." The congregation became much smaller as the men went about their tasks.

"Mr. Peglar, please board up the windows and doors as best as you can. I would like the men to be comfortable for a change," Sir Franklin ordered.

"I am able to help with that," Cassidy offered. The three remaining men looked astonished, exchanging astounded expressions with each other. "I'm positive it would make things easier, Mr. Peglar."

After some consideration, Sir Franklin finally responded, "If you insist, you can go with him. Irving, I want to discuss some concerns in private with you."

"Come along, Miss Cane, let's look at those windows and see what we can do with them." Peglar didn't wait for Cassidy. He was a good five feet away from her before her legs started to churn, she had to sprint to catch up to him. "Help me search for anything we can use to block the windows. I'd prefer not to use our own supplies, that will make it easier when we leave tomorrow." He sauntered towards a door; the stone had designs engraved into the archway. Peglar stopped to observe them. Perplexed by the illustrations, he turned towards Cassidy with a concerned expression on his face. "Have you seen these before?"

Cassidy leaned in closer, trying to detect any correlations with the Egyptian hieroglyphs she had spent years researching. The only connection she observed was the use of animals, but the characterization of bears and wolves dominated the carvings. "They appear to be telling a story." She discovered a logical sequence to the drawings. Wolves appeared to be in an eternal feud with a giant polar bear that walked on its hind legs. The bear had developed some traits of man, with its paws taking on the shape of hands and its defined musculature gave the creature a humanoid appearance. At the tip of the archway, a single stone had a disc-shaped object carved into it. In every image, every beast was bowed down in worship, with the bear above the disc and the wolves sprawled out in a circle. "Are these carvings on all the doorways?"

"We will have to look into that later," Peglar said as he pushed the door open. The cold, damp air flooded out of the room, wrapping its fingers around Cassidy. A tight spiraling staircase led down below, the dimness gave the impression of twilight in the absence of the glowing torches behind them. "Let's search elsewhere. I don't have time to go down there right now." Peglar closed the door behind him and shuffled over to the next room. Something in that place was calling Cassidy, imploring her to explore further. She turned back to find Peglar, who had already stopped to wait for her. "Are you coming?" he said impatiently.

Cassidy felt the urge to explore. Somehow, she knew something important was buried into the darkness of that room. "Just a second." She turned to glance over her shoulder, one last time, at the staircase before running over to join Peglar. She needed one of the torches from the wall before she could head down into the darkness. Peglar walked into another room; Cassidy took notice of the archway. Just stones and weathered markings, no hieroglyphics over this door, or anywhere else nearby. The former occupants filled the room with lumber and ancient wooden doors.

"Perfect, just what we are looking for," Peglar exclaimed excitedly. "I will fetch some men to carry over the boards." He pushed past Cassidy and wandered back into the great chamber.

Cassidy grabbed a torch from the holder on the wall and bolted towards the darkened passageway, eager to explore what lay beneath the castle. She closed the door behind her quietly, making certain not to draw attention to herself. Despite the brilliance of the flaming torch, the dimness of the staircase gave the impression of gloom, keeping its secrets carefully concealed. Carved into a solid slab of rock, the stairs spiraled downward into the madness below. The irregular steps and rough landings made it a hazardous descent. Cassidy couldn't see much further than a few steps in front of her. A musty, damp smell awaited her at the bottom of the steps, an encompassing layer of cold cut through her jacket. She was chilled to her soul. The bottom of the stairs led to an empty room, the light did little to illuminate the space, but she found torches hung in place along the wall. As she lit the first torch, the shape of the room came into view. It was a complete circle, Cassidy walked along the edge, lighting the torches spaced equally throughout the circumference of the room. Each torch lit illuminated a new detail that had been sheltering in the obscurity.

Now that all the torches were lit, Cassidy was disappointed to find that there was no other way out of the room but back up the stairs. Fully illuminated, the details carved into the floor virtually appeared out of thin air. It depicted an enlarged version of the hieroglyphics that decorated the archway upstairs on the floor. Except now all the images were centered around the mysterious disc. All the wolves appeared to be after the artifact and the bear-like creature was defending it. Slowly walking over to the center, she cautiously avoided stepping onto the disc. She took notice of the positioning of all the groupings of wolves; they mirrored the locations of major landmasses on earth. Centered in the middle, the disc marked the location of the magnetic North Pole. Was this drawing a map?

Accidentally stepping onto the disc, a low rumble moaned in the room. The ground started to shake and shift underneath her feet. Before she could run back to the stair, Cassidy felt the floor open up beneath her and she collapsed into the unknowing darkness below.

CHAPTER FIVE

Sharp pain radiated from her elbow and back, tumbling down the angled shaft left scrapes and bruises all over her body. Luckily, she had dropped out of the tunnel feet first, bracing herself against a painful fall. The torch had fallen on the ground behind her, but miraculously remained lit. The pale yellow light twinkled in the puddles collected in the gravel along the narrow passage. Somehow Cassidy avoided breaking any bones during her fall. She dusted off her clothes, realizing that she had several scrapes over both of her hands. With a heavy grunt, she bent down and massaged a knot from her back as she stretched out for the torch. An intense pain threatened to collapse her as her back muscles cramped. The torch weighed tremendously more than it should have, the burden to straighten up unbearable.

Cassidy looked up towards the hole in the ceiling, finding it pitch black. The light from the torch too feeble to shed its glow upon the trail. "Now what?" She murmured to herself, discovering herself in yet another avoidable situation. The walls of the underpass were black, jagged rock. Moss grew upon the surface all around, mushrooms sprouting up from the tiny cracks. As painful as it was, Cassidy twisted her neck to examine her two options. The tunnel led straight ahead in either direction, both paths looked forlorn. Disoriented by the fall, Cassidy wasn't certain which direction was north. She remained silent, evaluating her options. A delicate breeze rushed past her face. Barely noticeable, but just enough for her to distinguish which direction it flowed. She turned to face the breeze and began to wander down the passage. Condensation wet the soil beneath her feet, she watched the beads of water dripping down the rocks. With every passing minute, Cassidy could feel the current growing stronger. A low whistle began to form softly in her ear.

Grrrrrr

A low, deep growl echoed through the caves. It was too far away for Cassidy to determine its origin. Her heart started to race, pumping blood to her leg muscles, strengthening them to perform their next move. Curiosity, as it invariably did, got the better of her. Without hesitation, she proceeded down the narrow tunnel. Her only escape was to turn and run down an unexplored path, not sure what awaited her on the other side. With every stride she took, the light reached further into the uncharted, towards the source of the potential menace.

Rrrrrr

A guttural snarl froze Cassidy in place, the sound much closer than before. Vibrations of the low grumble trembled the ground beneath her feet. A stiff wind blew out the torch, casting her into seclusion. It took a moment for her eyes to readjust. A distant radiance from the end of the tunnel provided just enough light for her to find her way down the trail. The tiny dribble of sunlight had just enough influence over the darkness to guide her. Cassidy looked over her shoulder, finding nothing but darkness behind her. Forced to proceed forward, Cassidy found the determination to press on. Her heart pounded in her chest with anticipation. With every step towards the exit, the daylight's power grew stronger. The ground was dryer here than it was further into the grotto, the fierce bitter winds of the tundra lashed out at her. A reminder of the frigid temperatures awaiting her. Cassidy could see the pure white tundra just outside of the opening. A flood of relief washed over her, drawing her out into the opening.

The usual blustery noises of the tundra came to an unnerving halt. Not a single sound existed around her, Cassidy stopped still, the hairs on her arms rising in alarm. Silence replaced the boisterous wind, setting her on edge. A loud crunch in the snow echoed from the nearby forest, a branch snapped followed by a low, guttural grunt. She remained frozen, alarmed by the extraordinary, throaty growl rising around her. The sound was low and menacing, it filled the primal animal savagery with hunger. Another harsh growl ripped from the creature's throat as it sauntered out of the tree line and into view. A polar bear, standing on its hind legs, was taller than any man she had ever seen. Sharp, white daggers protruded from the creature's moist jaw. The creature's front paws crashed back down into the snow, sending a thunderous crunching sound booming across the desolate earth between them. The dying light of the sun captured in the creature's fur, giving the beast a yellow aura.

Cassidy didn't stand a chance in the deep snow against

the bear, she could scarcely maneuver in this untouched environment. She turned and raced back into the seclusion of the cavern. Blinded by the bright light outside, her ability to see in the dark was temporarily diminished. The low rumble of the bear as it raced across the tundra at her propelled her legs forward. She kept stubbing her toes against the craggy rocks. As she slowly pushed further into the cave, the low grumble of the bear approached rapidly, gaining ground on her at a threatening pace. Adrenaline fueled Cassidy's body, preventing her from tripping on one of the derelict rocks in her path, her legs pumping faster now. A faint flicker of light guided her. It was coming from far away, but it was all she needed. Cassidy squeezed through a narrow opening, forcing her slender frame through.

From the shadows, the predator appeared with a ravenous expression on his snout. Cassidy let out a shuddering gasp, she could feel the creature's warm breath from the other side of the tiny opening. She watched as the creature curled up its gums to reveal the stained teeth, letting out a low rumbling growl. Pacing back and forth, the polar bear beat its claws off the rock wall in frustration. Shards or rock scattered across the stony path below. Cassidy slowly started to withdraw, never taking her eyes off the fearsome predator. The bear let out one booming, angered roar before disappearing back into the shadows. Somehow, Cassidy knew that the creature wasn't done with her, she felt a curious attachment to the beast that she couldn't explain. After a few deep breaths, Cassidy remembered what had led her down this path. Quickly turning around, she saw the dancing torch light in the distance. It's flickering flames casting men's shadows on the wall. "Help!" Cassidy screamed out. She strained to hear a response, but none awaited her, she had to keep moving. Lost in some network of caves below the castle, Cassidy had never felt so alone.

With her arms outstretched, her hands braced her against the wall, the dim light guiding her towards her purpose. Every step allowed the yellow flame to illuminate the tunnel a little more, she could almost run now. She cupped her hands, "Hello." her voice rang softly off the walls.

"Miss Cane?" Sir Franklin's voice responded. Cassidy rushed forward; the harmony of his voice calmed her mind. She could see his shadow spread out on the cavern wall about one hundred feet in front of her. The narrow corridor opened into a larger chamber, she scrambled towards it. An empty void separated Cassidy from Sir Franklin, an ominous hole between them. "There you are."

Cassidy noticed the relief in his expression from across the void. A giant pool of water lay thirty feet below them, rugged rocks sticking out of the surface of the tranquil water. "How am I going to get across?"

"I don't know." Sir Franklin scratched his chin. "The gap appears too wide for any ladder we have. Have you explored the caves yet? Maybe there is another way out."

"There's a giant bear down here." Cassidy shuddered at the thought of the terrifying creature. "And I don't even have a torch." Her voice seemed to be swallowed by the water below, her words falling into the treacherous chasm. She looked around the room, the stonework that made up the foundation of the castle had seen better days.

The lack of sunlight and neglect had allowed large clusters of mold and algae to form. Bricks lined with cracks and chips poked out from underneath the blackened mold. The corners of the room lay in shadows. Sir Franklin began to pace along the edge of his path, allowing the yellow torch light to reach the corners of the room. Tucked away in the far-right corner was another passageway, a torch posted to the wall right next to the exit. With a jump in her step, Cassidy rushed over to the doorway. Only the rusted hinges remained, the door a distant memory to the space. As she picked up the wooden torch, spiders scurried away, disappearing into the algae. Cassidy had seen far worse in the caves in Egypt, the sight of the arachnids not bothering her.

"I will send my men outside of the castle to search for a hidden entrance." Sir Franklin shouted, his voice a distant echo.

All Cassidy wanted to think about was finding her way out of this underground network. "There is an entrance along the backside of the castle." Cassidy remembered. "You will need the shotguns. There is a large polar bear lurking about." Sir Franklin tipped his hat to her before retreating up the stairs to the main level of the castle. She stood in the darkness, trying to think of a way to light the torch. After several minutes of deliberating, she remembered what the elder chief at Gjoa Haven had placed in her pocket. She reached into her pocket to fetch the lighter. With a flick, a tiny flame sprouted up in the darkness. Damp cloth didn't make lighting the torch easy, she had to stand there for several minutes before the embers grew large enough to generate light. A set of stairs spiraling downwards waited for her. Echoes of the men's voices carried above her, their feet stomping around on the stone floors caused dust to fall from the ceiling. The low, gruff rumble of the polar bear sounded in the distance below.

CHAPTER SIX

Flickering glints of light illuminated brilliant high-lights etched into the wet stone walls. The pitch blackness below engulfed all the light from the torch, not allowing the light to penetrate it. Cassidy shivered against the seeping cold, her breath floated past her vision through her pressed lips. After having identified the exit to some elaborate underground network of tunnels, the echoes of men's voices faded. The staircase seemed to go on forever in a never-ending spiral. Every rotation around the center sphere brought her deeper into the frigid darkness. It threatened to consume her.

Etched into the walls, hieroglyphics of animals told a grand tale of some ancient battle or discovery. Dominant over all the animals, the polar bear appeared to be the guardian to the great disc. The prospect of solving this riddle distracted her from the growing coldness that enveloped her, penetrating through her furs and into her bones. Whatever that disc represented, Cassidy knew she would have to find a way past the polar bear. Thoughts about the creature's ancestry raced through her mind. Was this bear a direct descendant of the beast portrayed on the wall? Part of a long line of guardians? Was it the same bear?

At the bottom of the staircase, the splintered remains of a wooden door lay strewn about. Violent claw marks marred the fragments of timber. Cassidy walked over the abandoned remains of the door, forcing her way into the darkness. Somehow, the darkness seemingly sought to reach out and capture her, fighting against the pale yellow of the torch. Coldness surrounded her like a mausoleum. It was an overpowering sensation, far removed from anything she had ever experienced underneath the scorching dessert. The musty smell of moss and rich earth was heavy. Once she passed through the opening into the next room, she recognized the source of the earthly aroma. Bare earth replaced the stone and trees sprouted forth from the soil. High above the trees, a slight opening in the roof allowed sunlight to nourish the wildlife that called this cavern home. Birds fluttered their wings between the branches, flying amongst the trees, humming their soft tune. Cassidy stood in awe of this slice of heaven buried underneath an unforgiving tundra. Snow filtered in through the hole, falling harmlessly to the ground below. A giant pool in the middle of the cave had steam billowing off the surface. A natural hot spring providing warmth and shelter to everything dwelling in the cavern. Beads of perspiration began to form on Cassidy's forehead from the heat, her backside still chilled by the glacial climate of the castle hallway. She moved deeper into the cavern; the ground was soft, her feet sinking into the soil. The trees were all slanted towards the opening; they appeared to be reaching out for the sunshine. Taller trees near the middle blocked out the sun, the trees behind them got smaller as the darkness consumed them.

What lurked in the blackness?

Cassidy moved closer to the water, towards the origin of light. A beam of light appeared to be striking the ground just beyond the pond, on the other shoreline. A fish breached the water, the small arctic char made just enough noise to catch her attention. With lightening reflexes, a bird swooped down from its perch and plunged into the water with a big splash. It emerged from the water, the arctic char still wiggling within the bird's beak as it disappeared back into the tiny forest. Cassidy cringed as she heard the bones of the fish snap. She unzipped her jacket as she approached the warmth of the lagoon, embracing the change in temperature. The coldness left her body, gratefully replaced by the humid steam. Another splash rippled the waters on the pond. Cassidy stepped onto the muddy bank, her winter boots slipping in the muck. Crystal clear water filled the pond. Every detail was on display, the pond filled with varied species of fish. Speckled rocks and seaweed covered the bottom, a layer of slime built over everything.

Upon closer scrutiny, Cassidy realized that this body of water wasn't a pond. It belonged to an underground river, the current could be observed beneath the surface. Wildlife from the Arctic ocean passing through the covered rivers must stop here for a rest during their migration. She bent down to place her bare hand in the water, finding it much colder than she expected. With her cupped hands, she scooped up the ice-cold water and drank. Untouched by the influence of humankind, nature at its finest. The source of the heat wasn't coming from the water. It had to be coming from something else. Whatever source produced the heat, it wasn't coming from the lake. Something else in this cave was generating a tremendous amount of heat. All of that didn't matter right now, Cassidy allowed herself to bask in the warmth. As her entire body began to get back to normal temperature, she allowed herself to momentarily forget about the problems she faced. It allowed her to refocus, turning her attention to a solution. If she could climb one of these trees, it would be possible she would be close enough to exit this cave through the opening above. With any luck, the polar bear would still be hunting for her far beneath the castle and she would have enough time to get back to Sir Franklin's group.

With her neck strained, she looked up towards the exit. She was discouraged to find that none of the trees were close enough for her to make her escape. There was no way she would risk falling into the frigid waters from that height. If the fall didn't kill her, the ice-cold waters would finish her. Maybe there was another way out of this cavern. Another tunnel or escape route nearby, hidden in the darkness surrounding her. After several moments of deliberation, she determined the best thing to do for now was to examine the other side of the pond. She certainly wasn't in a rush to exit this warm cave and head back into the blistering cold. The edge of the pond was treacherous, her feet slipping in the slick mud. She headed back onto the grassy bank that bordered the pond. The ground was still damp here, but it was manageable. Every so often, Cassidy would notice animal prints in the softened ground. She bent down to inspect the paw prints.

Her heart leapt into her throat when she realized that she was looking at the imprint of the polar bear that had been stalking her. With giant claw marks that dug deep into the earth, the size of the paw amazed Cassidy. She stepped down into the print, the paw twice the size of her own foot, even with the winter boot.

Silence settled over the clearing. Birds stopped chirping. The water was deadly silent. A booming roar rattled the cave, the birds fluttered their wings and made a racket. Even though the grumble was far away, panic began rising in her chest. Her lungs constricted, robbing her muscles of the oxygen they craved. The realization of the monstrous breadth of the bear crippled her. Frozen in place, she awaited another thunderous growl to signal her demise. At any moment the alabaster bear would emerge from the darkness. Cassidy wouldn't stand a chance. For what seemed like an eternity, she stood still in silence. There were no more growls or groans. Slowly, the birds began to chirp. The rush of water trickled back into existence. Her thoughts escaped the panic that had taken hold, the muscles in her legs found the courage to keep moving. She laughed out loud, her hearty chuckle in cadence with the melody of the fowl.

With new-found energy, Cassidy rushed towards the sunlight. Snow falling through the cracks melted before it could touch the ground, the precipitation turning to rain. The light struck the ground just beyond her vision, the bank veering downwards just beyond the tree line. Once she stood at the edge, she could see down a stone structure at the bottom of the hill. The light shined directly into the building through an opening. She could hardly believe what she was looking at, the stone temple erected to collect the light from above. The bank was steep, but Cassidy didn't have the patience to find a better way down. With an agile leap, she pumped her legs to keep herself from falling over. Nearly tripping up in her own feet, she scrambled towards the stone wall of the temple at breakneck velocity. It didn't take long for the features of the stone to fill her view. She reached out her arms to brace herself against the wall; the stone was cold and slippery. Unable to stop herself with her hands, she used her forearms and shoulders to break her fall. The pain radiated up her shoulder and deep into her back. Cassidy cursed under her breath. Cold to the touch, the stones sent shivers through her body. The building stood about ten feet tall with a square base, styled in the fashion of a shrine. Something about the way they laid the rocks reminded her of the structures the Inuit built. Stones laid on top of each other, the same way they built the Inukshuk. Somehow, the structure was sturdy without the benefit of any bonding agent. The ground surrounding the structure was dried out; the grass burned down to the roots, Cassidy cautiously made her way around the side of the structure. She rounded the corner, the blackened caverns now to her back, an opening in the middle of the stones allowed entrance.

Cassidy eased her way to the doorway, not allowing herself to take her eyes off the darkness. With her back to the door, she stared at the cave wall. It reminded her of staring into a pitch-black night sky, void of any stars or moon. Oblivion, that's what it reminded her of. Serene sound caught her attention, she turned towards the opening, a gentle melody played from deep within the structure, drawing her into the sunlight. A comforting warmth embraced her, the pleasant aura of cardamon and ginger greeting her. Clay bowls laden with treasures rested along a ledge that ran the length of the entire room on all sides. The middle of the floor opened into a stairwell leading down, the beam of sunlight following the stairs. Dream catchers hung from the ceiling, dangling in the darkness. The light funneled through the opening above her, the beam intense and golden yellow shined brilliantly in the room. An extraordinary sensation of exhilaration washed over her, everything in the room was charming. The scent, the warmth and the beauty enticing her to explore further.

Enveloped by the refreshing environment, Cassidy closed her eyes and allowed herself to become absorbed in the experience. Something remarkable was waiting for her in this building, but that could wait just a little longer. She felt as if her wounds were being healed. Mental and physical exhaustion disappeared; the weight of the world lifted from her shoulders in an instant. It wasn't often Cassidy felt this euphoric; it was a rush of adrenaline and endorphins being released into her bloodstream. All she wanted to do right now was stay in this state of euphoria, lost in a momentary paradise.

ROOOOAAAARRRRR

The resounding roar violated the peacefulness of the room. Cassidy twisted around and confronted the opening, materializing from the obscurity was the polar bear. It raced towards her with prodigious velocity. White teeth protruding from the creature's jaw, it only opened its mouth to let out a thunderous grunt or deep snarl. Cassidy backed away helplessly, her only chance was that the creature could not fit though the opening. Before she could realize, her back foot didn't find any footing, and she tumbled head over heels. Everything spun around violently in her vision as she fell down the staircase. She reached out to brace herself, but her fingers slipped off the slick stairs and walls. Hitting the landing hard, Cassidy found herself staring straight back up the shaft. It wasn't as long as she thought; the fall taking much longer than it should have. Every bone in her body ached. Instantly, bruises started forming on her ribcage and legs. The ground rumbled as the bear galloped towards the stone structure. Cassidy held her breath and waited for the beast to appear at the top of the stairs.

BOOM

An exploding blast bellowed above; a faint flash lit up the room above her. The ground trembled as something above her crashed into the ground. She heard someone shouting something inaudible. A tall, black shadowy figure emerged at the top of the stairs. "Cassidy, is that you?" Peglar's voice cried out.

"Mr. Peglar," Cassidy responded with glee. Finally, she wouldn't have to run from that cursed polar bear any longer. Blood thirsty, the animal chased after her with conviction but without purpose.

"Are you alright?" Peglar started to walk down the stairs, the sunlight catching in the metal of the shotgun barrel.

Cassidy pushed herself up, forcing the muscles to work. "I'm a little sore but nothing serious." Cassidy brushed the dust off her trousers and jacket in an attempt to disguise her pain. Stiff and tense from the fall, her legs trembled beneath her. The thundering echoes of the polar bear's paws started up again. Peglar turned towards the sound and charged towards the noise, the shotgun raised to his chest in front of him. "Mr. Peglar," Cassidy yelled out, not wanting him to get hurt. No response, merely the sounds of the creature's gnarled roar and their footsteps echoing above her.

BOOM

Another roaring boom ripped through the cavern. Cassidy could feel the tremble in the ground growing smaller, but there was no crash this time. An anxious moment passed by quickly before Mr. Peglar appeared once more. "The fool got away, but he'd be a bigger fool to come back." Mr. Peglar held up his weapon with satisfaction. He scrambled down the stairs with grace, the slippery surface no match for his agility and steel-spiked boots. "I only grazed the beast, but I think he gets the message."

"I hope so. That thing has been chasing me since I fell through the floor." Cassidy choked back a tear, filled with relief and grateful for the presence of Mr. Peglar. Awkwardly, he stood in front of her. He didn't know how to acknowledge the quiver in her voice. Cassidy took a moment to regain her composure. "We need to explore this structure."

Fear shrouded Peglar's features, a deep terror pouring from his eyes. "This place is cursed." he shook his head, "we need to leave now." He reached his hand out and nodded his head towards the exit.

Cassidy took a step backward. "No, there's something

down here and I need to discover what it is."

"There's nothing down there but misfortune and sorrow." Peglar hushed his tone. "There's a reason the people who lived here built this place. They had to make certain that no one else ever stumbled upon that evil creation."

"What are you talking about?" Cassidy questioned, softening her voice to match his. She took a step forward, they huddled close together. "If it's so evil, why didn't they just destroy it?"

"I'm talking about something from another world. The last time they tried to destroy it, terrible things happened." Peglar's voice shivered with dread. He was uncomfortable being so close to the source of evil. "The only thing they could do was bring it here and try to ward off the curse."

"How do you know it's cursed?" Cassidy needed to learn as much as possible about the artifact. If she was going to find it, she preferred to understand what she was dealing with.

"Sir Franklin's father discovered it during his expedition to find the North West Passage. They had got caught in the ice north of King William land. Once they recognized they weren't going anywhere, Sir John Franklin sent a crew out in search of land where they could take refuge from the storms." Peglar's voice was filled with apprehension. "The men don't remember where they were when they discovered it, but they mentioned being stalked by a polar bear the moment they took it into their possession."

"The same polar bear that has been trailing me?" Images of the hieroglyphics rushed through her mind. A polar bear was guarding the artifact from the wolves — were mankind the wolves?

"Your guess is as good mine, but they say that bear tormented the crew. Sir Franklin maintained the metal disc held tremendous capabilities and refused to abandon it. Half of his company committed mutiny, many perished during the struggle for power. It forced those that remained to abandon the two ships in the ice."

"What was the name of those ships?"

"The HMS Fear and, Sir Franklin's ship, the HMS Erebus." Peglar answered. A realization that this world was bound to her own shook Cassidy to the core. Sir Franklin's failed expedition had gone unexplained for over a century. The recent discovery of his sunken ships only added to the mystery. Many people had once believed the thick Arctic ice smashed the two ships, but both ships were discovered unscathed. Both ships were located far from where they had been abandoned. "Sir Franklin held onto that disc until the bitter end, convinced it would benefit humanity."

"What made him so certain?" Cassidy was intrigued by Mr. Peglar's every word. This ancient mystery was intriguing, filling her with conviction. She needed to solve this mystery.

"No one is sure. They came across a village of Inuit people. When they discovered the device, they informed him it had been left behind by the people who came from the sky."

"Do you mean aliens?" Only Cassidy Cane could feel this much joy located so close to an artifact filled with ancient alien machinery.

Peglar paused for a moment, perplexed by the question. "Alien?"

"People from another planet," Cassidy said matter-of-factly.

"What other planet? We have never seen people from another planet." The question troubled Mr. Peglar, he responded as if she had insulted him.

"Just continue your story, forget I said anything." Filled with regret, Cassidy craved to learn more about what happened to Sir John Franklin's crew.

"The Inuit people told him that the artifact needed to be transported back to where they found it and buried. Mankind was not ready for the powers left behind by the sky people. Once they were ready, the artifact would help salvage mankind." Mr. Peglar gazed into Cassidy's soul, his eyes fixed on hers. "In the right hands. If the disc falls into the wrong hands, it would be a powerful weapon." He examined her, as if inspecting her. "Why are you so resolved on discovering what rests beneath this room?" Peglar raised his voice, making sure she heard his every word.

Not knowing what to do, Cassidy decided her only option was the truth. No benefit would come from trying to make up a lie. "I have been sent here from another dimension." She expected a shocked expression on Peglar's face, but he remained stoic. "To retrieve the artifact for a scientist in another realm. A dimension not unlike your own."

"You're the one the prophecy spoke of." Peglar continued to study her, looking for some unknown sign. "Perhaps you work for the evil forces spoken of by the Inuit."

"I can assure you, I'm not evil." Cassidy almost laughed at the notion, she may have been a lot of things, but evil? Certainly, she was adventurous, but never evil.

A hearty laugh escaped from the belly of Peglar. "Miss Cane, I have no doubt that you are nothing but virtuous."

"Then what's so ridiculous?" Cassidy joined in the laughter.

"You don't see it yet, do you?"

"Get what?"

"Who sent you here?" Peglar stopped laughing.

"Doctor Herbert Gamgee," Cassidy explained.

"And how well do you know this man?" Peglar pressed the question.

This wasn't the first adventure she had been on for the doctor. "I've worked with him before." Maybe she let the thrill of his missions cloud her judgement. "I don't know him much beyond that. His motives are a mystery to me."

"Have you ever thought that his intentions are not for the greater good?" Peglar paused, looking deep into her eyes. "Is he the prophesied evil the Inuit spoke of?"

CHAPTER SEVEN

"I honestly don't know." Cassidy pondered Peglar's question. Unable to think clearly, she had doubts about what would happen next. "All I know is I need to find the artifact." Driven by the rush, she would worry about the next step once she arrived there.

"I won't stop you," Peglar said with compassion. A deep, implicit understanding between the two. "But I won't go down there with you. I will wait for you here." He held out the shotgun to her. "Do you know how to use this?"

"I've fired one a long time ago." Cassidy remembered the bruise that had formed on her shoulder after firing the weapon. The kickback of the gun nearly breaking her collarbone. "I don't need it." Cassidy pushed it away from her.

"Are you sure I can't persuade you to take the shotgun with you?" Peglar held the gun firm in his hands. "I'd feel a lot better knowing you have protection."

Cassidy shook her head. "I really don't want it. Besides, if that polar bear comes back, you will need it. To protect us both."

Peglar nodded in agreement. "If you insist. Just holler out if you need my aid. I won't leave until you come back up. Be careful."

"You too."

Cassidy turned around and walked down another set of stairs. The sunlight fading into the obscurity, the torchlight flickering off the walls. The stones vanished into the natural rock that formed the network of caverns. Someone had taken the time and effort to burrow deep into the earth, smoothing the walls as they descended. Before the sunlight completely faded, Cassidy turned to face the top of the stairs. It was comforting to see that Peglar stood watch over her. Darkness waited for her beyond an arching doorway carved into the rock. She crept past the entrance, finding a narrow path in front of her. The edge of the rocky path dropped off abruptly. Cassidy could hear waves roaring beneath her. The dynamic force of the Arctic current remained invisible but felt as the crashing waves smashed against the rock wall. Salty sea air occupied the room with a briny smell, it was so dense she could savor the ocean on her tongue. Cassidy noticed a kerosene lamp hung from a hook. A luminous flame erupted in the glass lantern as she passed the flame of her torch underneath the opening, casting light further into the cave. Lanterns had been placed around the room. She trudged along the path, igniting the beacons along the way. A single rocky pathway stretched out into open water. The emerald-green water only ten feet below. Drops of water splashed over the path as the waves broke on the rock face below, the ocean slowly eroding the narrowed pathway.

Darkness hid the path, the passage continuing on into

the misty abyss that seemed to stretch on into eternity. Rocks fell into the water below as Cassidy transferred her full weight onto the path. The roar of the waves drowning out the sound of the rocks entering the water below. She peered over the edge; the whitecaps of the waves rolled past. The raging waters had chiseled a tunnel through the rocks and passed through the other side, time had created an unstable bridge. As she wandered further from the safety of the shore, Cassidy became more determined to find where the path led. The artifact she was searching for remained entombed in the shadows. Beneath her feet the stones trembled. Every step brought her closer to the end of her quest. The flickering light of her torch revealed a metallic object nestled on an alter about twenty feet away. Adrenaline flooded her body. Her legs compelled to purpose, she dashed down the path. Raw energy emanating from the plate vibrated through her body. The alter carved from the rock with hieroglyphics etched into it.

Cassidy stood in front of the alien artifact, close enough to reach out and touch it. Deep down inside, she realized she should turn and flee. Something else was compelling her to reach out and touch it. A force beyond her own comprehension, more powerful than anything she had ever experienced. Without reason, she reached out and picked up the metallic artifact. It was heavier than it looked. The disc fit in her palm, its surface ice-cold, yet it emitted a tremendous source of heat. It pulsated pure energy through her body, she wanted to throw the disc into the waters below, but it wouldn't let her. She couldn't explain the sensation, she placed it back down on the altar. The immense surge of electricity left her body the moment she set it back down on the altar. She grabbed her pair of gloves, hoping that thin fabric would somehow protect against the unexplained power. A low, growing rumble rattled the chamber. Rocks cracked and broke off, falling into the emerald waters below. Something beneath the water began to rise from the depths. Before Cassidy could see what it was, she snatched the artifact, surprised to find that the electrical surge was dampened by her winter gloves. It was still present, but it no longer consumed her body. She tossed the foreign technology in her pocket and dashed across the bridge as quickly as she could. A deafening boom knocked her down, nearly sending her into the water below. She stared down at the waters below. The emerald liquid swirling into a violent vortex, sucking in large hunks of rock as it grew in size. There was something in the eye of the funnel, rising from the crevasse.

A hand grasped her jacket, yanking her to her feet. "We must leave this place." Before she could see who her saviour was, he was steering her towards solid ground. They ran as fast as possible, the rock bridge crumbling beneath their feet. She could feel the path swaying beneath her feet, ready to disintegrate into the glacial waters below. A boisterous, piercing screech tore through her skull. The sound trying to freeze her in place. As they reached the edge of the bridge, they both leapt just as the bridge crumbled into the ocean below. Cassidy landed on solid ground. Her guardian angel was not so lucky. She twisted around to find a hand desperately clutching the side of the path. A figure developed from the water, the waves carrying it towards them. Cassidy reached out and snatched the man's hand just as he lost his grip, his weight dragging her closer to the edge. She stared down at Mr. Peglar, his panicked eyes staring back up at her. The shotgun was grasped tightly in his hand, he refused to let it go. He dug his boots into the rock face, taking the burden of his weight off her shoulder. She got to her feet, the floating figure drawing closer as she pulled Peglar up with all of her might. He tumbled on top of her as she wrenched him over the edge.

Peglar leapt to his feet, pumped the action of the shotgun and took aim at the mystical creature closing in on them. A deafening boom burst from the shotgun, an intense spark illuminating the complex underground cavern. The figure riding the waves wasn't slowed down by the blast. It was closing in on them now. Slowly, the features came into view. Tall and elegant, the mysterious figure took the form of a woman. Her onyx hair danced in coils around her round face, her tanned skin free of blemishes. Big, walnut brown eyes stared down at them, her pouty brown lip curled upwards at the corners. Peglar pumped the shotgun once more, raised it to his shoulder and took aim. "Stay back," he yelled in vain, the woman hovered just a few feet away from the ledge. Peglar turned to face Cassidy. "Run you fool." Fear rattled his voice, his entire body trembling.

Cassidy stumbled to her feet and darted forward, grabbing ahold of Peglar's winter slops. She dragged him towards her, urging him towards the exit. "Come with me." He fought against her grip and freed himself. "I'm not leaving without you."

Peglar turned towards the woman, the wave inching

closer to the shore. Her arms outreached for them. Cassidy knew she was reaching for the artifact, she sensed the woman's gaze upon it. The disc in her pocket surging with electricity, sending waves of heat coursing through her body, her muscles engorged with strength. She reached out once more, grabbing Peglar by the elbow and hauling him backwards. Her newfound strength shocking herself and Peglar, he tripped over his own feet as she yanked him. She caught him before he fell and led him towards the exit. After a few steps, Peglar decided to join her rather than struggle against her will. Cassidy entered the tunnel first, her feet skipping every second step as she raced up the stairs. The pulsating alien disc providing her with a source of unbridled power. Peglar's footsteps echoed closely behind. Rays of sunlight above marked the exit, guiding her back. She raced through the carved archway and burst out into the open cave, the earthly smell of soil and moss greeting her immediately. Her chest heaved up and down as she struggled to catch her breath, the artifact ceased to provide energy. Peglar exited the stone shack behind her, bumping into her, and sent them tumbling to the ground.

"We aren't done yet." Cassidy got to her feet first, presenting her hand to Peglar and dragging him to his feet. He nodded in agreement and slung the shotgun over his back. The woman was crying out to them, her shrill voice filling the cave. A flurry of wind threatened to drive them back into the temple. Cassidy felt a shockwave of heat erupt from the disc, forcing back the windstorm. Opportunity reared its head, and a slab of ice dropped from the ceiling and landed on the stone structure. In an instant, the man-made building imploded, sending a wave of dust and debris flying in all directions. Destruction and pandemonium reigned all around. Defeated shrieks cried out from beneath the caved in structure. Cassidy heard the thunderous pounding of the polar bear's paws in the distance, approaching them. Likely drawn in by the commotion. Somewhere lurking in the dark, the howl of a pack of wolves rose. "What are we going to do?" Cassidy jumped to her feet, not knowing what problem to deal with first.

"I remember the way out, follow me." Peglar took her by the arm and guided her towards the shadows. The shotgun gripped firmly in his fist, bounced off his hip as they ran.

They sprinted down the bank, the growing sounds of howling wolves surrounded them. Movement caught Cassidy's eye, a pure white wolf dashed across her vision and dissolved in an instant. Torchlight reached the darkness, a pitch-black hole in the cliffside stood out. Cassidy knew where they were going and raced ahead of Peglar, her long strides carrying her towards the entrance. The body of another wolf darted towards them from the left, quickly gaining ground on them. Another two wolves appeared out of thin air from the right, the pack had surrounded them and cut them off. Both of them halted. Peglar raised the shotgun in the air and fired off a round. A shower of ice and rock pelted them from above.

The thunderous boom momentarily scared off the wolves, they retreated into the shadows, buying them enough time to escape. Without hesitation, they ran into the cave. The torchlight couldn't reach the walls of the cave as it gave way to a large opening. "Now what?" Cassidy said with a sense of urgency, discovering herself lost in the open space.

"I think it's this way." Peglar pointed into the darkness. It all looked the same in every direction. A high-pitched howl startled Cassidy. She turned to see the pack of wolves had followed them into the cavern. Peglar pointed the shotgun in their direction and fired another round. The wolves scattered in different directions. "That was my last shell," he said, frustrated.

"Let's hope they don't know that." Cassidy tugged at his sleeve and looked him in the eye. "What way do we need to go?"

Peglar spun around, trying to find his sense of direction once more. He oriented himself with the door, trying to make sure he was composed. "It's this way, I'm sure of it." He guided her off into the darkness.

CHAPTER EIGHT

They hurried through the cave as fast as their legs would carry them. Sounds of paw prints gathering on the rocky floor growing louder behind them. Wind threatened to blow out the shimmering flame. Cassidy followed close behind Peglar, his winter jacket making loud flapping noises as he ran. Out of cartridges for the shotgun, they were running out of options. Cassidy heard the wolves sniffing the air, their wet jaws snapping at the scent. The cavern was a never-ending black void, no matter how fast they ran they couldn't find the edge. "Are you sure this is the way?" Cassidy called out to Peglar.

"I'm positive," Without turning his head, he responded. His voice carrying into the void, no echo returned. Peglar was breathing hard, his laboured breaths growing deep and saturated with fluids.

Cassidy wanted to race past him; his pace was much slower than her own. The only reason she didn't take the lead was the faith she placed in him. She believed that he knew the way, but doubt was clouding her judgement. "Hold up." With a swift burst, she ran ahead of Peglar and spun to face him. "I can race ahead to check."

"There's no time. The wolves will be upon us in an instant." Peglar was frightened. "We need to stick together if we are to stand a chance." Every word had to be forced out between choked breaths. His chest was expanding rapidly. Beads of sweat dripped off his skin. Howls from the wolves rose behind them, precariously close now. Claws digging into the rocky terrain could be heard tearing into ground. "We are almost there."

Peglar led the way, convinced that he was heading the right direction in this black abyss. There were no identifying features to guide them. Only the pale light from their torch to accompany them, they advanced through the darkness. Cassidy ran alongside Peglar now, the urge to dash forward grew greater. She couldn't elude the wolves. Their only chance was to arrive at the exit before those wild animals cut them off.

"We are almost there." Peglar pointed to the shadows. Cassidy strained her eyes, the wandering shadows playing tricks with her view. At the boundary of the light, she saw a wall of rock leading straight up. As they drew closer, a staircase heading up began to form. Adrenaline flooded into her body, giving her a boost. A tiny chuckle escaped her lips, she was too happy to contain herself. She reached out and grabbed Peglar by the elbow, rushing him along with her. Her heart leapt into her throat and she let out a terrified gasp. A single white blur rushed past the staircase, then another crossed its path. Peglar stepped in front of her, protecting her from a frontal assault. She pirouetted around only to discover more wolves. Their circle was getting tighter, closing the distance between them swiftly.

"What do we do now?" Cassidy wasn't ready to give up.

Peglar bent his knee and picked up a handful of rocks, cramming them into his pocket. "We have to act quickly." He gestured to the ground. "Grab as many as you can. We are going to get as close to the staircase as we can before we start to throw the rocks at them. With any luck, we will have just enough time to make a break up the stairs." Cassidy bent over and scooped up a handful of rocks. They were cold and wet, the jagged edged poking her through her gloves. Peglar turned towards her and placed his hands on her shoulders. "Listen, no matter what happens to me you run as fast as you can. Don't wait for me and don't do anything stupid. Do you understand me?" The wolves edged closer; they slowed their movements now. The gaps tightening along the perimeter. Peglar shook Cassidy back and forth. "Do you understand?" A tear rolled down his cheek.

"Same goes for you," Cassidy snapped back. "Don't think you need to be the hero." She palmed a rock and closed her fist tightly around it. "We are running out of time." She brushed his arms off his shoulder. He thrust his hand into his pocket and pulled out a large rock, nodding his head in agreement. All around them, the wolves bared their teeth and snapped their jaws. They lashed out at them with low, guttural snarls. The growls rumbled from deep within the pits of their bellies.

In unison, they both dashed towards the staircase. Cassidy took aim at the wolf closest to the stairs and threw the rock with all of her might. It landed in front of the beast, the resounding bang startling the creature.

It dashed out of formation. Peglar let his rock fly just after her, his projectile much more accurate. It found its mark, banging into a wolf's head, sending the creature scurrying away whimpering. A gap big enough to run through opened up and Cassidy broke into full stride. She reached the stairs and turned around. A wolf was nipping at Peglar's jacket, he turned around and took a swing at the critter. His blow caught the creature on the side of the head. The wolf recoiled away, baring its jaws at Peglar in defiance as it backed away, its head dipped low. Cassidy threw her rock towards another wolf approaching Peglar from the left. It struck the creature in the rib cage, stunning it long enough for Peglar to make a break for it. Cassidy threw another rock in his direction, the loud banging clap providing just enough distraction for Peglar to make his escape. He joined her on the stairs and didn't wait for her to turn around, he spun her around, nearly knocking her off balance.

"We have to keep moving," Peglar screamed as the wolves regrouped. The pack approaching the stairs cautiously. Cassidy threw her last rock into the pack, striking one wolf. It let out an agonized yelp, but the wolves were not defeated yet. They scrambled up the steps together. Cassidy skipped steps but she wasn't as sure-footed as Peglar, her feet slipping out from underneath her. Several times, Peglar had to catch Cassidy before she lost her balance completely. Peglar turned to throw his last rock at the wolves, who were already making their way up the stairs. His throw missed the lead wolf but sailed into the pack and struck another square in the snout, causing him to yelp in torment. The angered howl of the alpha male rallied the others, coaxing them to proceed despite the peril.

"What way do we go when we reach the top of the staircase?" Cassidy noticed the ledge just ahead.

"Turn left and run towards the light." Peglar was falling behind, gasping for air.

Cassidy turned and ran down to yank Peglar forward, she would not let him give up so easily. "Keep your legs moving." With a handful of dirty fabric, Cassidy pulled Peglar up a stair. That seemed to ignite a fire in the older man, his limbs started churning again. For the first time since they entered this cave, Cassidy felt the disc in her pocket. It began to resonate, a slight pulse that beat faster as the wolves got closer. She didn't want to wait to find out what would happen if they got too close. A strange sensation began to throb in her abdomen. Fear, that was the only word Cassidy could think of to describe the feeling growing inside of her. Was this pulsating a warning, an omen? Something told her she had to keep the disc away from the wolves at all costs.

After a few laboured leaps, they reached the top of the ledge. Together, they both turned left and raced towards the torches that marked the exit. "We are almost there." Peglar pointed to a black iron gate. It hung open, swaying with the breeze lazily. The light from behind giving the illusion that the iron bars were growing and shrinking in size.

"Get inside." Cassidy rushed forward, racing to the gate. She grabbed ahold of the cold iron bars, waiting impatiently for Peglar to enter the room before she closed the door. The wolves were nipping at his heels, the back of his foot catching the jaw of the alpha. A painful expression crossed Peglar's face as he let out an agonized cry in unison with the wolves. The impactful blow causing both of them to suffer injury. Cassidy slammed the gate shut just as Peglar crossed the threshold. The alpha wolf leapt into the air, throwing its body against the gate in a vicious act, knocking Cassidy backwards. She fell hard onto her backside, straining her neck to monitor the gate. Peglar struggled with the door as he tried to close the latch. Stunned from the impact, Cassidy could only watch as the wolves pounced towards the door. The pulsating artifact in her pocket let out a high-pitched, piercing wail that cut through the tunnel. The wolves dipped their heads down, covering their ears with their paws. Cassidy jumped to her feet and latched the lock.

The sound ceased; the defeated growls of the alpha wolf pierced into her soul. It paced back and forth, trying to find a weakness in the gate. The obedient pack continued to toss their bodies at the iron, the alpha watching attentively for any hint of weakness or default. "Come, let's put some distance between us before they break the gate down. It's only a matter of time before that happens." Peglar pointed to the roof where the iron cut into the rock, the bars were shaking. Debris and dust falling from the ceiling. The alpha wolf was staring at the same thing, frothing at the prospect.

Peglar ushered Cassidy further into the bleak hallway, the carved tunnel diving deeper into the earth. Loud, crashing bangs erupted behind them as the wolves continued to throw their bodies into the iron gate. "How much further is it to the castle?" Cassidy wanted to take her mind off the disturbing sounds behind her. She needed a distraction, anything to help her ease her mind.

"We still have a way to go." Peglar's voice echoed loudly in the tunnel. "This is the sub-basement of the castle above. It is a network of passageways. A man would easily become lost down here."

"Luckily, I am not a man, and I don't plan on getting lost down here." Cassidy laughed, hoping to ease the tension.

"No one ever plans on getting lost." Peglar chuckled. "It just happens sometimes." They walked into an intersection. Peglar studied the markings on the wall. Cassidy couldn't make any sense of the words written there. It appeared to be some kind of code written in another language. "We have to go left."

"How do you know that?" Cassidy stared at the markings. Some carvings were words, some of them were symbols. Each wall had their own combination.

"Those are common nautical terms, and the symbols represent truth or lies. Sailors during the war came up with the codes to deceive the enemy. If they captured a ship, the captors wouldn't understand the orders they found." Peglar walked down the left corridor, the sounds behind them fading. A solitary wolf howled into the tunnel one last time before they put enough space between them.

"When did you learn about all of this?" Cassidy allowed her mind to wander. The path was ice cold, but the disc in her pocket acted like a furnace, providing enough heat to keep her body temperature comfortable.

"During the great war." Peglar's voice was distant, he

stared off into the distance, looking past the cave and into the past. "I was a boatswain on Sir Franklin's ship during my time in the military. After two years of war, I had been lucky and never had to fire my weapon. I had directed my skills towards other pressing matters."

"What do you mean?" The tunnel forked left and right, Cassidy studied the markings again. They looked very familiar to the ones at the last junction, only a slight variation to the carvings.

"Which way do you think we should go?" Peglar questioned her, avoiding the question.

The drawings had to be the key. She recognized the nautical term for left and right, the trick would be determining the symbols for truth and false. "Should we go left?"

"We should, but can you explain why?" Peglar attempted to teach her.

"Are you avoiding the question about the war?"

"Yes, I don't like to talk about the war." Peglar didn't hide his intentions.

"I don't understand why I chose left." Cassidy wasn't ready to let the subject go yet. "Why don't you like to talk about the war? You said you never fired your weapon."

"There can be worse things than killing a man during war." Peglar responded as he turned down the tunnel. "I'll give you another chance at the next junction to crack the code."

"If I crack the code, can you tell me what happened?" Cassidy kept pressing.

He stopped in mid stride. "If you explain to me how the code works, I will tell you. Not a guess, I want the explanation."

Cassidy held out her hand. "Deal." They shook hands in agreement, a deal brokered between them in the cold pits of the castle. "If you don't want to tell me, you don't have to."

"I will tell you," Peglar spoke softly. "It's not something that I can hide from you forever. Other people understand what has happened to me. It is no secret amongst our crew."

"Then why not just tell me?" Cassidy didn't understand his attempt at secrecy.

"Just because it's not a secret, doesn't mean that it's easy to talk about." Peglar quickened his pace. His entire body trembling beneath his winter jacket.

"Are you okay?" Cassidy asked, concerned. She reached into her pocket and held the alien artifact in her hand.

"I'm just a little cold. All of that running caused me to overheat and sweat. Now that I'm not running, my body temperature is still adjusting. I'll be all right in a few minutes, just need time to acclimatize." Peglar's lips started turning blue, his teeth chattering. His cheeks had turned a pasty white.

"You don't appear well. Are you okay?" Concerned for his wellbeing, Cassidy took the disc out of her pocket. "Take this, it should keep you warm." She handed him the disc. He happily took it from her hands, holding it close to his chest. A soft smile spread across his face. "Does that help?"

"It does." Peglar unzipped his winter slops and placed the disc inside a pocket. They continued walking down the corridor. The curved ceiling covered in frost, the floor slick with ice. Their pace slowed, every step a dangerous adventure for Cassidy. She struggled to gain any traction on the black ice. "Here we are, your final test. Which way should we go?" The tunnel opened into three different directions and wooden signs hung from the ceiling marking each corridor.

Cassidy studied the words carefully. Starboard, port, and head were scribbled on the signs leading left, right, and straight. That part was easy, all the words matched the direction. It was the symbols that didn't make much sense. Three anchors rested beneath each word; those were identical. It was what was wrapped around the anchor that differentiated them. Beneath starboard, the anchor was wrapped with a rope knotted at the top. Underneath head the rope was also knotted in the same fashion but the rope was frayed. The last knot, underneath port, was tied to the right and the rope was free of any defects. "I know that the ropes have something to do with it."

"Very good, you are headed in the right direction," Peglar emphasized the last word, placing a great deal of theatrics with it.

"The knot for starboard is the only one that isn't facing the right direction, so left is incorrect because it's not true?" An educated guess, but still a shot in the dark. Cassidy studied his expression for any sign that she was headed in the right direction. Peglar said nothing, he just nodded his head. Not in agreement, he just acknowledged her heard her. "The other two knots face in the right direction, but the rope facing the head is frayed. You wouldn't want to use that rope, so it is false. We have to take the path on the right, because the rope and knot are true." Cassidy was sure of the answer. Peglar stood stoned faced, hiding a smirk stretching across his expression. He let out a tiny chuckle. Annoyed by him, Cassidy stomped her feet. "Well, am I right?" she demanded.

"Miss Cane you are a very intelligent woman. Perhaps your husband served, and you paid attention to his tales?" Peglar saw the angered look on Cassidy's face. "I meant no offence. I just never experienced this before."

"Experienced what? A smart woman?" She spat back, insulted by his comments.

He shook his head. "No, Miss Cane, I've never seen anyone solve the code so quickly. You are correct, we head down that path." His words were jovial, a look of pride on his face. The same look a teacher has when one of their students accomplishes something great.

"Well, I've held up my end of the bargain, what happened to you during the war?" Cassidy was still upset, her blood boiling.

"Nothing."

"Nothing? That's your big secret?" Cassidy sensed her face flush red with anger. "Why would you hide that?"

Peglar began walking down the tunnel. "If you ask any of the men in Sir Franklin's crew about their experience during the war, they will have something to tell you."

Cassidy picked up the pace, glad to get moving again, the chill was seeping back into her bones. "I don't get it. What are you hiding from me?"

"Miss Cane, I am not hiding anything." Peglar turned his head to face her. "I am ashamed that I never experienced action. The others returned home with tales of bravery and victory," his said, his voice laden with regret. "When I arrived in my home, I had nothing of worth to mention. Even though I never shied away from the action, I was never placed in a position to prove myself." He was no longer talking to Cassidy, his internal monologue spoken aloud for his own benefit. "No one ever called me a coward, they never needed to. Everyone knew that was the only logical explanation. How else could a man avoid such hardship during a war?"

"That is nothing to be ashamed of." Cassidy truly believed those words. War was a terrible thing. It created terrible demons that could ruin people, destroying everything in their path. She had seen families destroyed by the experiences of combat. Peglar remained silent, ignoring Cassidy as they trudged down the path. "You mentioned your skills were utilized elsewhere?"

"I became an expert at navigation. I studied the patterns of ice and how to survive in the frigid conditions." Pride lingered on his tongue, but it was burdened by his shame.

"So, you became an Ice Master, that is a very important position aboard any ship." Cassidy remembered reading about the position in a book she studied in college about the Franklin expedition.

"It is important during times like these." Peglar responded sharply. "Not during a war. The only reason for my position aboard this ship is because Sir Franklin feels sorry for me. He believes that I can still be useful but everyone else would just as soon cast me overboard, they hate taking orders from a man like me."

Every footstep echoed loudly, almost obnoxiously in

the silence. The wall creaked, the ice in the cracks expanding against the stone in an extended battle for position. Without another word spoken, they walked down the long hallway, the moaning of the castle creating an eerie atmosphere. Mother nature had taken residence here, her cold touch decorating the hallways with sheets of ice. At the end of the hallway was another junction. The signs that should have been hanging from the door had fallen onto the ground, and ice had formed over them. Peglar stood over the signs and shook his head. "Damn it, they fell face down."

"So what do we do now?" Cassidy could hear the panic in his voice.

He kicked his spikes into the ice, the hard surface suffering minor scratches but refused to give any ground. "We will have to make a guess. I don't remember which way I came down here."

"Let's take a minute to think this over. Maybe something will jog your memory." Cassidy remained calm. "Was the tunnel very long?"

"I remember it took me a fair amount of time to walk down the first tunnel, if indeed this is the last junction." Frustration clear on his voice. "This damn disc has lost all of your body temperature and has gone cold again." Peglar took the artifact out of his pocket; the metal had lost its lustre. The light no longer catching on its surface, he held it out for her to take.

Cassidy reached out and took ahold of the disc. Instantly, the surface shimmered again, the dull light of the torch dancing across the metal. "That's weird." Cassidy felt the disc spring to life, a warmth spreading through her veins the moment it was in her possession. "It's warm."

Peglar reached out and placed his hand on the artifact. "That is most peculiar." He stared at Cassidy with great interest. His lips opened to speak, but he was drowned out by a terrible crashing sound. They both jumped, startled by the sudden commotion. "What was that?"

ROOOOAAAARRRRR

A booming growl responded, answering the question. The trembling echo was much too deep to belong to the wolves. Peglar stared at Cassidy with a fear in his eyes. They looked down the three tunnels, not know which way to go. Neither of them knew the correct path. Thunderous galloping shook the tunnel as the polar bear rushed into the underground network.

"Run."

CHAPTER NINE

Their footsteps were drowned out by the pounding paws chasing after them. They ran into the darkness at full speed. Already twenty feet ahead of Peglar, Cassidy had to slow down so he wouldn't be left behind in the shadows. Cassidy heard his laboured breaths from the edge of the torchlight, struggling to keep up with her. A pulsating throb grew stronger with every step she took deeper down the tunnel. If it was a warning, it was too late, there was no time to turn around, they had to keep pushing further into the underground network. She slowed her pace enough to allow Peglar to catch up. "You have to keep up, we are almost there."

"This doesn't seem right," Peglar choked out between panting breaths. He had discarded the shotgun somewhere behind them, the weapon no longer in his possession.

"Just keep your legs moving," Cassidy tried to sound reassuring, but the booming paws were drawing closer. Grunts and groans from the polar bear closing in on them. The intensity of the disc increased; a sense of dread crept over her. "We will get out of here."

Peglar staggered forward, unable to keep moving in a straight line. Wasted effort, Cassidy did her best to keep him on track. Her leg muscles were cramping, depleting electrolytes leaving her vulnerable to exhaustion. The tunnel opened into another junction. Without speaking another word, Peglar grabbed Cassidy by the shoulder and dragged her into the right path. The signs rushed by too quickly for Cassidy to read. Peglar's laboured breaths betrayed their position, panting loudly he buckled over. "I need a moment." He stopped moving, bending over at the hips he dry heaved.

"No, we can't stop." Cassidy pushed him forward. "Keep moving, no matter what, don't stop moving those legs." Cassidy dug her shoulder into his side, helping take some weight off his legs, they staggered down the long tunnel. The snorts and grunts grew louder, closing in on their position. The polar bear, sniffing at the air, following the lingering body odour directly towards them. She expected any moment to turn around and witness the creature lumbering down the tunnel. The pulsating disc grew stronger, the energy radiating an undeniable power that couldn't be ignored. Cassidy noticed another junction straight ahead that only had two paths. "Left or right?"

"I say we go right." Peglar was still trying to catch his breath.

Cassidy felt the ground beneath her feet tremble, the polar bear was dangerously close now. They only had one chance. They entered the junction and began to turn right. A stabbing pain forced Cassidy to one knee on her left side. Peglar stumbled over her, collapsing into a heap in an effort to avoid falling on top of the smaller woman.

An anguished cry escaped her lips. Something deep inside was telling her to turn left. "We have to go the other way."

Peglar got to his feet first, pulling Cassidy up from the ground and taking the torch from her hand. "Then we will go left."

The sharp pain ceased, and Cassidy continued trudging along. The whole tunnel trembled as the polar bear let out a deafening roar, rattling the surrounding walls. As they passed the junction, Cassidy caught a glimpse of the enormous beast's white fur glowing from the darkness. Fear propelled them both forward with newfound purpose, their legs ignoring the fatigue. This tunnel differed from the rest. It twisted and turned, bending left then right as it weaved its way upwards. Fresh air rushed past them as they pushed further into the tunnel. "This has to be the right way." Cassidy's heart leapt with joy. Peglar kept pace even as he struggled to catch his breath. The path sloped upwards now at a sharp angle, the ice giving way to the stone path beneath. Tremors shook the tunnel, the bear's growls rumbled from the pit of its stomach as it chased after them. Cassidy was too afraid to turn her head, she just kept her legs churning towards the exit.

"No," Peglar screamed in anguish. The flickering light reached a dead end. A stone wall greeted them at the end of the path. "This can't be."

"Wait, I think I see a hole." Cassidy found a black opening, situated near the bottom of the floor. They continued to race towards the wall, their only chance of survival was hidden within that tiny hole. A gust of fresh air was billowing from the hole.

"Get in, I'll be right behind you." Peglar forced Cassidy into the small tunnel first. It was pitch black and covered in ice, the tight confines of the tunnel constricting her movements. She crawled on her hands and knees, dragging herself forward into the darkness.

Peglar screamed bloody murder behind her. Contorting her body into a painful position, she watched him crawling towards her. He had dropped the torch outside the tunnel, the faint light catching in the polar bear's pure white fur. Claws digging at the walls in a furious attempt to widen the hole, the creature desperate to follow them into the abyss. "Keep going," Peglar cried out in pain. With all of her weight on her forearms, Cassidy pulled herself forward, dragging her body behind her. Someone had carved the tunnel out of the ice, making it difficult to gain any traction. Her elbows digging painfully into the ice, she kept moving forward as fast as possible. Peglar was following close behind her, his hands bumping into her feet as he pushed himself forward.

Cassidy was warmed by a trickle of sunlight in the distance. "We are almost there," Cassidy said joyfully, a renewed source of energy driving her forward. "We made it, Mr. Peglar."

There was no response. Only the frantic clawing and throaty growls of the bear at the other end could be heard behind her. She twisted her body, barely able to see past her own waist. Desperately, she forced her body to one side to allow the tiny amount of light to illuminate the cave. Peglar laid face down in the tunnel, his jacket had been torn from his body. "Wake up, Mr. Peglar." Out of frustration, she kicked his arm. His chest was still moving up and down rhythmically, she kicked him again.

"Just…" Peglar croaked. "Go on without me."

"What is wrong with you?" Cassidy pleaded. "If you keep moving, you will warm up."

The bear was tearing away at the ice, the hole widened enough to let the creature stick its shoulders through at the bottom. His claw dangerously close to Peglar's feet now. Painfully, Peglar crept his body further out of the rabid creature's reach. The sickening sounds lashing out at them. Shards of ice fell onto the stone path behind the bear as he tunneled his way into the ice. "Don't worry about me." Peglar coughed. "Just go."

Cassidy refused to take her eyes off him, driving herself closer to the exit with her heels. A low murmur drifted into the cave. The sounds coming from the exit. "Help!" Cassidy screamed. "We're down here."

Silence.

"Down here."

Mumbles filtered down to her. She couldn't pick out the words, but she knew they were voices of Sir Franklin's crew. "Mr. Peglar needs help." Cassidy turned to make sure he was still following her. Even though she had only moved ten feet, he wasn't able to keep pace. He was falling behind, his face buried into his chest. Desperate to keep warm, he had forced himself into the fetal position. "Please, we need your help."

"Miss Cane." A young man's voice finally answered. His frame blocking the light from the exit.

"We are in here."

"Hold on, I will get you out." Cassidy recognized the voice. It belonged to Tommy Seeley.

"Please hurry." Cassidy forced herself back towards Peglar. He was barely moving now, his efforts wasted. "We are almost there." Cassidy assured him. He didn't respond, his breathing was shallow. "You can't quit now." She grabbed him by the shoulders, dug in her heels and pulled with all of her might. All of her effort only moved him a few inches, but she refused to let go, straining again, she pulled him even less with the second attempt. Her face bright red from exhaustion, she tried to get a better grip. The bear snarled and grunted as it clawed away at the ice, a constant reminder of the threat just below. "I need help," Cassidy called out to Tommy.

"I'm on my way." Tommy's voice seemed more distant now than before. She turned her head to confirm he was in the tunnel. His outline was slowly making its way towards her. More voices erupted in the background. Frantic sounds of commotion loomed ahead. Dreadful, demonic sounds inched closer from below.

"You have to hurry," Cassidy frantically cried out. The vicious growls below frightened her to the core. Peglar's weight was threatening to pull them back down the tunnel. A powerful, clamping mouthful of teeth eagerly awaiting them. The hot stench of devoured meat oozing from the rabid jaws below, pouring over them.

Cassidy gripped Peglar underneath the armpits, planted her feet and tugged with all of her might. She dragged him for several feet before the white stars appeared in her vision. The surrounding commotion began to blur together, fading into white noise. She braced herself once more, pulling Peglar another foot. Her head began to swim, the stars clouded her vision until all she could see was a single, bright light. Cassidy tightened her grip as she felt consciousness slipping away, refusing to give up. Unable to pull him any more, she locked her grip underneath his arms to make sure she wouldn't lose him.

Cassidy blacked out.

CHAPTER TEN

The tunnel was narrow, a slight slope leading up-wards taxed Cassidy's leg muscles just enough to make her groan at the effort. A radiating tingle warmed her back, the raw energy from the disc vibrating through the pocket that had fallen over her back. The polar bear's roar echoed behind her. The mighty bellow booming off the tight walls, enclosing her in boisterous noise.

Cassidy Cane stared at the elderly man, his ice-cold blue eyes and alabaster hair gave him the appearance of a ghost. The long furs draped over his frail frame hid his shaking arm that rested on the mahogany wood cane. In his younger years the man stood head and shoulders above the crowd, but now he hunched over at the hips, barely able to meet eyes with her. She held out the ice-cold metallic disc, the radiating source of energy smothering all of her senses. "What is this?" She demanded.

"I will explain that to you if you wish, but there is so much more that you need to understand." His voice was raspy, each word barely escaping his dried lips.

"I don't have time for games. What is this?" Cassidy's heart was still beating wildly in her chest. A raw surge of power waxed and waned in her hands, a pulsating beat that mimicked the rhythm of her own beating heart.

"That is a source of pure, clean energy." The elderly man made his way towards a small, rounded wooden table. He pulled out the wooden chair, the four legs scraping across the hardwood floor. "Please join me, my legs aren't as strong as they once were." He used his cane to push out the chair.

A flashing image of Mr. Peglar crossed her vision. "What happened to him?"

"Please have a seat." He tapped the chair with his cane, the rattling noise pounding in her skull.

She refused to take a seat. "You have to tell me what happened to Peglar." Cassidy crossed her arms across her chest in defiance.

"Tea?" The old man pushed a white porcelain cup across the table towards her.

"How d'you do that?" Cassidy found herself sitting across the table, she wanted to stand up, but her muscles didn't respond to her brain's demands. Instead, she reached out and took a sip of tea. It was warm, and it replaced the coldness from the tunnel.

"I can assure you that Mr. Peglar is safe. Thanks to your heroic actions, he will live to see another day." Strands of the man's white beard flowed over his neck, his Adams apple bobbing beneath. With shaking hands, he sipped on his tea, the cup clattering against the plate as he placed it down. "That is not why you are here."

Cassidy noticed the sway of the ocean beneath her. It didn't make any sense. "Where am I?"

"You are where you need to be," he stated calmly, not

answering the question. "What is critical is that you comprehend why you are here."

Cassidy recognized those words from earlier. "You are the man from my dreams." The elderly man let out a chuckle, his sly smile curling the long hairs on his lip. "That is not what I meant."

A raspy cough stuck in the man's throat. "I know, it's just not very often this old man gets to listen to a young lady say those words."

"Why am I here?" Cassidy leaned forward across the table. "And I don't want any cryptic answers this time. Please, cut to the chase." Subconsciously, she had grasped the tea and took another drink.

"Search deep within yourself. You should recognize who I am by now." His ice-blue eyes glared through her.

Frustrated by the elderly man's cryptic response, Cassidy banged her fist on the table. "You're Sir John Franklin." Unknowingly, the words spilled from her mouth without thought. "You were the first to discover this disc." She placed it on the table. His ice-cold eyes melted, revealing a deep brown iris beneath. "What is this?"

"Have you spent much time studying the Inuit folklore?" John Franklin's hair turned jet black, the wrinkles disappearing from his skin as his youth returned to him. "Have you ever heard the tale of the god who created the Tuurngait?"

"Yes, the goddess Sedna, the Spirit of the Sea sent the Tuurngait to kill the Spirit of the Air and the Spirit of the Moon. Tuurngait is capable of travelling between the spirit world and the physical world. After a battle with the Tuurngait lasting 10,000 years, the Spirit of the Air and the Spirit of the Consciousness work together to defeat it. The defeated Tuurnbgait attempts to defeat its creator, but the Spirit of the Sea banishes it to the physical realm." Cassidy had listened to the tales told by the elders during her stay at Gjoa Haven.

"That's correct." His voice was filled with youth now, it was strong and steady. "They say that when the Sedna vanquished the Tuurngait to earth, she lost her powers during the conflict. Her ability to harness the power of the sun lost, giving birth to the moon."

"Is that what this disc is?" She reached her hand out, the metal surface responding to her touch.

Sir Franklin noticed the strange reaction. "I have never seen it do that before." He reached out, disappointed to find it had no reaction despite his desires. "You must be the prophet. Your ability to manipulate the disc will be a great benefit to mankind."

"I did not come here on some mystical quest." Cassidy felt insignificant next to the artifact now. "That disc is not for me."

"What are you planning to do with it then?" Sir Franklin stood up, his frame broad and his chest thick with muscles.

Cassidy stood up in defiance, banging her fists against the table. "I didn't ask for this. My job is to bring this artifact back to Docter Herbert Gamgee."

"Did he tell you his purpose?" Sir Franklin bellowed; his words had enough power behind them to knock Cassidy back into her chair.

Cassidy thought long and hard. She still wasn't sure of the doctor's motives, but she had no reason to deny his request. "No, he did not. All I can say for certain is that the disc does not belong in my hands." Doubt muddled her thoughts. Was this just another adventure for her, or was this her purpose? Was she brought here by some higher calling?

"I need you to think long and hard about what you are doing." Sir Franklin snatched the disc up from the table. "I sacrificed over one hundred and twenty men to save humanity. If this falls into the wrong hands, the power it contains would be devastating." He tossed the disc into her lap.

"What would you have me do?" Cassidy clasped the disc in her hands.

"I would have you wake up." He pounded his fist against the table.

Cassidy jumped up in her bed. She awoke to find herself lying in a berth aboard a ship. The ocean tossing the boat back and forth like a child's toy. Her body was wet with sweat, and it took a moment for her heart to slow down and to gain her breath. "It was all a dream?" Cassidy said aloud, not knowing where she was.

"You are still dreaming."

Cassidy leapt up, tossing the sheets onto the bed. Sir Franklin was sitting in a rocking chair next to her bed. "What are you doing in here, Jack?" Cassidy reached for the blankets, pulling them up to her chin.

"Jack is my son, I am John." Creaks and groans filled the room as the chair rocked back and forth. "Like I said, you are still dreaming. You need to wake up."

"What does that mean." Cassidy wanted to scream. She was so frustrated she started to pinch the skin on her arm until she drew blood. "I just want this to end."

"Do you know why that disc reacts to you the way it does?" John asked patiently as she continued to pinch herself.

"I don't know anything about this…. thing." The artifact was underneath the cover with her, she felt it resting against her leg. "I just want you to tell me."

"You want me to tell you?" Sir Franklin chuckled. "You realize that I am a figment of your imagination, right?" He leaned in close to her. "The answer rests deep inside of you, just let it out."

With a balled fist, Cassidy took a swing at Sir John. Somehow, she missed hitting his face from less than six inches away. "I can't do this anymore. I'm done." She whipped the covers off, tossing them over Sir John. The blanket crumpled up into a ball in front of his feet, never once landing in his lap even though it should have. The disc sat in her lap, she stared at the shiny surface. Disgust contorted her expression, her nose crinkled up, sending a wave of wrinkles over her face. "It's because it belongs to my world."

Sir Franklin nodded his head in agreement. "You realize that if you bring it back to your dimension, that anyone could harness its powers."

"This disc can help solves the earth's energy crisis." Cassidy muttered to herself, refusing to talk to her subconscious any more. "Can it be weaponized?" She asked herself, remembering the immense power it was capable of producing. It had allowed her to escape with no knowledge of its capabilities. What if the wrong person got their hands on it? This disc could create something far worse than a nuclear weapon. The atomic bomb would fail in comparison to the raw energy surging within this artifact.

"In the wrong hands this source of energy could be used for terrible things." Exactly what Cassidy was thinking, John's voice seemed faded and distant.

"I don't believe Doctor Gamgee is the wrong person." Cassidy didn't expect an answer. "I should just throw that disc back into that cave and leave it there." Her head was spinning now. "But if he solved the world's energy crisis, it would change the fate of our planet." She couldn't decide what to do. "What do I do?" Cassidy screamed into an empty room.

"Wake up."

CHAPTER ELEVEN

Laboured yelling and frantic footsteps roused Cassidy to consciousness. She wobbled back and forth; the clouds gathered above her head. She strained her neck just enough to turn her head to the side, the wooden walls of a skiff greeted her. "Where am I?" Cassidy's throat was dry, the words catching in her larynx. Ice scraped the bottoms of the skis as she was being pulled away, the castle looming over her as they left. Men were screaming out to each other, the wind blurring their words together. She turned her head to the other side. "Mr. Peglar."

Peglar was lying down next to her. Unresponsive, his body bounced and twitched to the will of the sleigh. Every bump and dip rocking his body back and forth. His chest was rising slightly, the movement barely noticeable underneath the blanket they had thrown over him. A winter jacket and been thrown on him hastily. Cassidy looked down, surprised to find her fur jacket had been removed and replaced by the black winter slop that all of Sir John Franklin's men wore. Purple blotches filled her vision. A constant, throbbing headache made every movement agony. She wasn't able to concentrate long enough to pick out what the men were shouting about. Dried, cracked lips, made worse by the biting cold, made it nearly impossible to speak.

Muffled cries stuck in her throat as she attempted to call for help. She forced her arm to move her hands into her pocket. Agonized by the effort, her fingers searched for the disc. They ran across the cold metal, unable to tighten her grasp on the object. Burdened by the responsibility of retrieving the artifact back to her own dimension, Cassidy mustered her last ounce of strength. "Help." Scratchy sounds that resembled her voice crossed her lips.

"Hang in there, Cassidy, we will get you back to the ship safely." Tommy Seeley's voice appeared from thin air.

Unable to locate him, she decided it wasn't worth spending the energy, he would come to her. "Water." All she could muster was a single word. Anything more would have choked her. She felt a hand cradle the back of her head, tilting it just enough so she could receive a drink. The cold metal lid stung her lip, but it was worth it. The water was graciously received by her dry mouth, the moisture bringing her tongue back to life. It hurt to swallow, each gulp getting slightly more comfortable. "More water." Her throat no longer resisted the words. Tommy leaned in but his smile didn't last. A booming echo forced him to take action, he ran off towards the action.

Deep, heavy moans spilled out of Peglar, his limbs slowly coming to life. Then he rolled himself onto his side. He opened his eyes, dried tears stained his checks, he mouthed the words "thank you," no noise left his mouth. With newfound energy, Cassidy rolled onto her side to face Peglar.

"You're welcome." Cassidy reached out, placing her hand on his shoulder, she laughed. They had been through hell together. Barely escaping the clutches of the polar bear, they had been placed onto one of the skids to be pulled across the ice like luggage. She reached back into her pocket, finding that the object she believed to be the artifact was the barrel of a pistol.

Peglar saw the look of fear in her eyes, he reached out and seized her by the shoulder, restraining her from sitting up. "No." Dry orders delivered from his cracked lips, his eyes seeking to console her.

Cassidy dropped the pistol, thrusting her hands back into the pockets, hoping they concealed the artifact deep within. Empty. "I lost it." She brushed his hand away, forcing herself to sit up.

A dying yellow sun was minutes away from falling beneath the mountains. Dark, heavy clouds loomed overhead, the wind pushing them across the horizon. The barren tundra was cluttered with men accompanying the skid in a long line. Tommy Seeley was running towards her, an expression of dread on the young man's face. "Wait." Cassidy called out as he rushed by. The other men began to rush forward, moved to purpose by something unseen to her. There were no shadows to hide in.

The snarling growl of the polar bear sent shivers down her spine, chilling her to the core. "It's the bear." Cassidy glanced at Peglar. "It's coming after me." Cassidy turned her head and watched in disbelief as one sailor fired a shotgun at the bear. The slug knocked the animal backwards momentarily, the pellets falling into the snow harmlessly. The great polar bear reared onto its hind legs. There was no sign of blood anywhere on the creature's pristine fur. Cassidy turned her head forward as the sled jolted onward.

The men weren't running away. They were rushing forward to help pull the skid with the men in the harness. Men grabbed the ropes, dug their heels into the packed snow and helped. They toiled relentlessly, the skid moving along the snow much faster now as the weight was evenly distributed between the whole crew. The sails of the HMS Fear bobbed up and down in the distance. Wind caught in her sails, rushing the ship dangerously close to the ice. Sir Jack Franklin was leading a group of men towards them, every man armed with a rifle. War cries rose from the men as they raced forward to greet the bear head on.

A clap of thunder rocked the ice. White lightening tore the sky in half. Loud cracks rang out from the ice beneath her, the brewing storm threatening to open up the frozen sheets. The polar bear roared in defiance of mother nature, standing on its hind legs and thumping its chest with its giant clawed paws. The deafening roar challenged the clouds, which countered with another thunderous bang. A bolt of lightning struck the ice between them, sending fragments flying in all directions. A white cloud of fog, ice and water remained between them. Sir Franklin and his crew rushed past the last of the men pulling the skid. They took a knee, aiming their rifles towards the last known location of the bear. A booming rumble erupted from the sky as the men readied their weapons. The polar bear emerged from the mist, galloping full speed at them.

"Fire," Sir Franklin barked the order. Gunfire erupted, flashes sparked from the guns as another bolt of lightning illuminated the sky. Smoke seeped from the barrels, the wind driving it back in the shooters' faces. The polar bear grunted in defiance, baring its teeth at the soldiers. A flash of lightning illuminating the white skin, giving the creature the appearance of an ethereal glow.

"Retreat," Sir Franklin bellowed. His men raced to catch up with the skid. The bear followed closely behind, showing no effects from the gunfire. Not one bullet had penetrated the creature's thick skin. "Reload." Another booming clap quickly followed the command. The bear's claws dug into the snow, flicking up the shredded ice behind it as it barreled towards them.

A blinding flash struck the ice just beyond the skid, the powerful impact shifting the ice all around. Cassidy felt the skid tipping over, she did her best to brace herself against the fall. The sheet of ice hurtled towards her face as she was thrown from the skid, protecting her face with her hands. She slammed hard onto the ice, skidding across the surface like a ragdoll, stopping inches from the edge. The roar of the ocean just below. She inhaled the salt water below, its perpetual power pounding the ice.

"Fire."

Thunder drowned out the sounds of the rifles. A pair of hands pulled Cassidy to her feet. "Hold on tight." Tommy Seeley was holding a rope, squeezing her around the waist.

"What are you doing?" Before Cassidy could say another word, Tommy leapt over the ledge. Chaotic, swirling waters raged below. The grip of gravity tugged at

Cassidy's legs as they swung over the open waters. She screamed out loud until the solid wooden boards of the deck appeared underneath her. Pure joy filled her body as her feet touched the wood, lifting away the fear. Cassidy watched as the other crew members took the leap of faith, soaring across the gap defying the roars of the bear.

"I can't believe we escaped that polar bear." Joy overwhelmed Cassidy. The last crew members boarded the ship as the polar bear reached the edge of the ice. A bolt of lightning silhouetted the bear's dominating figure as it stood defeated. A mighty bellow left its belly, the resounding roar rivaling the thunder.

"That was no bear," Tommy said fearfully. "That was Tuurngait."

CHAPTER TWELVE

"Where is it?" Cassidy demanded, slamming her fist down on Sir Franklin's mahogany desk.

"You mean the disc?" He reached into his desk drawer. "Here, take it." He treated the object like it had a terrible curse, flinging it at her in one swift motion.

Cassidy caught the disc as it bounced off her chest. "You don't want it?" After all the tales that had been told, surely someone would desire it.

"The Tuurngait will hunt you down." Sir Franklin tapped his fingers on the metallic surface. "It will not quit until it has taken possession of it." He backed away and sat behind his desk. Bags had formed under his eyes, the events of the previous day robbing the captain of any sleep he was owed. "My father had buried it away, the inukshuk he built warding off the evil spirit."

"What evil spirit?" Cassidy questioned.

"The Tuurngait," Jack spoke, lowering his voice. "It will swim after us, following the mystical trail left behind by the disc. No matter where we run, we will never escape it."

"Why can't we just build another inukshuk?"

"My father had the help of the elder shaman. With his magical abilities, they warded off the Tuurngait." Sir Franklin leaned back into his chair, the wooden legs groaning underneath him. "My father fled your dimension, hoping to escape the Tuurngait's persistent pursuit. He couldn't close the dimension fast enough, the Tuurngait followed him through."

"What if I take it back to my world?" Cassidy knew after all of her adventures, if there was a way to stop the Tuurngait, Doctor Gamgee would figure something out. If he didn't already. The doctor always seemed to know more than he let on. "Then you wouldn't have to worry about that demon anymore."

"You would take responsibility for this terrible creature?" Sir Franklin didn't sound convinced. "Don't you understand that you cannot simply kill this creature by ordinary means?"

Cassidy didn't know if she could trust Doctor Gamgee completely, but she understood him well enough to realize he would stop at nothing for self-preservation. If she brought the artifact to him, he could harness the powers it contained and defeat the Tuurngait. "You have to trust me. Bring me back to where you found me. My escape pod should be somewhere in that harbour now. The Tuurngait will follow me back to earth and you will no longer have to deal with it."

"Very well. We shall set sail for Franklin Harbour. We should be a few hours ahead of that terrible beast by now. It's not the fastest swimmer, but it never quits. The longer we are searching for your vessel, the more danger we put ourselves in."

"It will not take us long to find what I am looking for." Cassidy chuckled at herself.

"Why would you say that?" Cassidy's light heartedness did not amuse Sir Franklin.

"I assure you, you've seen nothing like this." She winked at him.

Sir Franklin snapped his fingers. "Steward," He bellowed, his voice deep and authoritative. A young sailor entered the room, standing at attention just inside the doorway. His head was bowed to his chest, the young man's face riddled with acne and dry skin. "Tell Sir Irving that we are to change course to head into Franklin Harbour immediately."

"Aye aye, Sir." The young sailor clicked his heels and ran back into the hallway to carry out his duties.

"We should arrive shortly. If my estimations are correct, we are just passing the mouth of the harbour." Sir Franklin stood up, looking out the port window. A slight smile curled the corner of his lips. "Sir Irving tells me you are a Slipstreamer. He recognized that fact the moment he laid eyes on you."

"Why didn't he do anything?" Cassidy pondered. "I remember being chased one time by people who disliked Slipstreamers. I was caught."

"He said nothing because we are all Slipstreamers aboard these ships," Sir Franklin explained. "We had trouble with the people in this world. That is why we stick to the Arctic region. They do not care for it and we don't have the capabilities to battle them. They leave us alone, mostly."

"Mostly?" Cassidy laughed, remembering recent experiences.

"It lifts the spirits to view such splendid sights."

"Is Franklin Harbour your home?" Cassidy asked, unable to see anything but the white clouds in the sky.

"Most of my crew claim their homes in one of the many villages of this harbour." Sir Franklin continued to peek out of the tiny opening. "I am relieved to find Ice Master Peglar reporting for his duties. We had believed the man too far gone to be brought back to us. Yet he stands just two days after the torturous ordeal."

Cassidy rushed out of the room and ran down the hallway. She burst through the door, the salt sea breeze greeting her. "Mr. Peglar," Cassidy called out, relieved to catch him on deck. He turned to greet her, a joyous smile on his face. Cassidy ran across the deck and embraced Peglar. "You are looking much better."

"Much better thanks to you, Miss Cane." Peglar squeezed her elbow. "Tommy told me you never let go, even when he discovered you unconscious in that ice cold tunnel. If it wasn't for you, I would have succumbed to the bitter cold in that tunnel."

"I wouldn't be here if it wasn't for you either," Cassidy recalled the numerous times that he had saved her life. "What are you doing out here on deck?"

"The men spotted an odd piece of ice bobbing alone in the water. They called me out to have a look at it." Peglar pointed to port. "The ice is see-through, like glass."

"That is not ice, Mr. Peglar." Her heart leapt into her chest.

"What is that thing?" Peglar scratched his head.

"That is my way back home." Cassidy wanted to celebrate. "Bring us alongside, I have work to do."

"I will go tell Sir Irving at once." Peglar limped away.

Cassidy leaned over the rail, the winter winds pelting her face with pellets of freshly frozen water from the tips of the waves. The sun died in the sea's darkness. Tiny pieces of ice surrounded the wooden boat, the side of the ship scratched up from the frozen boulders. The howl of the wind drowned out the sounds of the water splashing against the gunwales. A low rumble rattled the decking of the ship as a miniature iceberg smashed into pieces against the side of the HMS Fear. Cassidy could feel the artifact surge with energy, it too, realizing that it was close to heading home.

CHAPTER THIRTEEN

Cassidy stared down at the panel, probing for the knob she had been trained would bring her back to the portal. The artifact rested heavily in her lap. She wondered if the artifact was trying to bring her back home, the extra weight trying to sink her towards the swirling portal hidden in the abyss below. Green, the button she was looking for was green. The memory of her training popped back into her mind. "There it is," She found herself speaking to the artifact, expecting it to communicate with her.

Silence.

Her finger pressed the button. A mechanical buzzing sound filled the compartment, the sea slowly rising, swallowing the capsule whole. The image of the HMS Fear fading out of sight, the dark waters enveloping her as she sank towards the bottom. It didn't take long before the portal reached out, grasping the sinking vessel in its clutches. The pod started to spin head over heel, as the currents pulled the device downwards in a tightening spiral. Immense force pinning her in her seat as she swirled around the vortex, the rotations spinning faster and faster as she neared the portal. Cassidy closed her eyes and waited for the nauseating sensation to dissipate. The artifact pressed down into her lap, the metallic surface radiating heat, the pulsating growing more intense.

Suddenly, Cassidy felt weightless, the force of the spiraling vortex disappeared. She opened her eyes, a dark void greeting her on the other side of the window. Surrounded by nothing but her thoughts, Cassidy anticipated another feverish dream. All of her senses were meaningless here. Touch, taste, smell and hearing rendered useless by the passage between dimensions. She had no control over them. Unable to recognize anything, drifting through the portal aimlessly. Time stood still. She didn't feel cold or anxious, she only existed in this portal. Questions raced through her mind, there was no time to answer them. What if the Tuurngait couldn't be stopped? Should she have brought this artifact back to earth? Did she trust Doctor Gamgee? Was she doing the right thing? What was going to happen to the people living in the other dimension?

The world exploded to life around her. Dark, purple waters gushed over the glass. The mast of the HMS Terror appeared in her vision. Bubbles of air raced her to the surface, the mast falling out of view below her as her pod launch towards the surface. Water rushed by, changing colour as the light reached into the depths to greet her. The force of gravity returned, pinning her into her seat with tremendous pressure. Her stomach turned over, the velocity giving her the phenomenon she was riding a roller-coaster, bursting out of the surface. Water splashed in all directions as the pod breached the surface. Cassidy landed back on the surface of the water with a hard thud, sending a terrible shot of pain up her spine.

It was dusk now, the horizon purging the sunlight into dying flames, the last of the day's heat all but gone now. Bitter cold flooded the cockpit. "Damn it." Cassidy pounded the heat, demanding that it turn back on immediately. She fiddled with the toggle frantically.

"You are back with us, Miss Cane." A voice appeared over the crackling receiver. Bright light emitted from the dashboard as the power surged back to life. Heat began to filter through the vents as the electricity turned back on. "I will have the rescue team extract you from the surface immediately."

"Doctor Gamgee?" Cassidy couldn't pick out the voice over the static crackling.

"The one and only," Gamgee acknowledged. "I assume that you managed to uncover the artifact."

Cassidy wasn't absolutely certain if she was ready to hand over the artifact. How much time would she have to dispose of the disc, and what would happen if the Tuurngait found it? "Yes, I have it," Left with no choice, Cassidy admitted that she had it. "But there's something I need to tell you."

Before Cassidy could respond, Gamgee's voice interrupted her. "I assume that the Tuurngait followed you here. I have measures in place to deal with that creature."

"You knew about that." Cassidy was furious. "Why didn't you warn me about the Tuurngait?" Her face flushed red with anger.

"If I told you about the creature, you would not have gone after the artifact." Gamgee tried to defuse the situation.

Only infuriated by his response, her blood pressure began to rise. She scanned the console for the switch to open the glass covering. Tempted to throw the artifact into the frigid depths, her finger levitated just about the toggle. "I might have died. That creature was relentless. It nearly killed one of us." With a jolt, the glass slid open. A gust of wintery air swept over her, expelling all the heat from the compartment in an instant.

"I had faith in you." Gamgee remained calm. "I still do. I know you won't toss that disc into the ocean. So why don't you close that glass dome and stay warm. We are prepared to handle this."

"How can you tell that the dome is open?" Cassidy blurted out. Shivers took control of her body, she couldn't stop herself from shaking.

"We can see you." A bright flood light shined across the water from an approaching vessel. "Just hang tight, we will be there in just a few minutes."

Cassidy sensed a presence rising from the depths. The disc went crazy. An energy overload spilling from its surface caused the disc to turn bright white. Cassidy looked over the side of the floating pod. An ethereal, alabaster glow was swimming towards her. "It's here," Cassidy tried to call out. Fear gripped her by the throat, asphyxiated by the words as they stuck in her larynx. She watched in horror as the form took shape, the massive limbs of the Tuurngait taking shape in the depths. Gnarled claws stuck out from the creature's enormous paws, gashing at the water as it swam towards her. "Help me." Cassidy was helpless.

"Like I said, Cassidy, we are prepared." Gamgee's

voice echoed from the radio.

Tuurngait erupted from the waters, leaping onto the edge of the pod. Its tremendous weight driving the nose of the vessel to submerge. Water flowed over the ledge, splashing onto Cassidy's legs. Frantically, she scurried towards the aft, desperately trying to escape the vicious snarl on Tuurngait's snout. It stood on its hind legs, letting out a thunderous growl towards the sky.

A flash of green light pounded into the Tuurngait's chest. Paralyzed by the emerald light, Tuurngait fell backwards into the water. The ship rocked back into place as the creature's weight dispersed. The boat puttered alongside the mighty creature, casting an ivory-coloured net over the Tuurngait. The mechanical winches struggled to pull the Tuurngait out of the water. "What are you doing?" Cassidy called out, trying to warn them.

"We have what we came for now." Doctor Gamgee appeared at the side of the boat, his black toque pulled down to his eyebrows and a neck warmer pulled up to his nose.

Cassidy threatened to toss the disc into the frigid arctic sea. "You don't have it yet."

"Oh, that thing, you can do whatever you want with that. I've said it before, Cassidy, I came prepared, and I possess what I wanted." Gamgee motioned towards Tuurngait.

Cassidy didn't know what was happening. "Here, this might be useful too." She tossed the disc at his feet.

Greedily, he bent down and retrieved it. "I will be able to save a lot of lives with this, Cassidy. You've accomplished the extraordinary this time."

Cassidy was cold and tired. All she wanted to do was rest, her part in this was finished. "Just get me out of here." Gamgee motioned towards his crew, who threw a ladder over the side of their boat. Quickly realizing that his plans were far beyond anything Cassidy dreamed to comprehend, she reached out and climbed the ladder. Standing in front of Doctor Gamgee, she watched him place the artifact inside a steel crate before slamming the lid shut and locking it.

"Well, Doctor Gamgee, what are your plans for that creature?" All Cassidy wanted was the next adrenaline rush, she didn't think he was going to spill the beans on his plans.

"I plan to study this magnificent creature. If the anecdotes about it are genuine, it was conceived by the Inuit gods," He spoke excitedly. "Within the genetic structure of this creature I may find the cure for cancer, or any number of diseases."

"What about the disc, you must know of its capabilities to harness extraordinary power?" Cassidy was surprised by Doctor Gamgee's forwardness. She didn't expect an answer, maybe she could probe further into his plan and set her mind at ease.

"I heard the stories, yes." Gamgee nodded his head. "What I have not learned is how I will be able to utilize the powers contained within. Perhaps the answers to all of my questions lie within the Tuurngait. Perhaps the answer lies in another dimension. We must keep searching them."

Cassidy embraced the adrenaline pumping through her veins already. "Where to next, Doctor?"

EPILOGUE

Tallis ran, his black hair bobbing on either side of his head, as a barrage of laser fire followed him. His breath was hot and humid, pushing out into the cold air and becoming vapor that trailed along either side of his head as he ran, like steam coming from a train.

He was wearing a large fur coat over his shirt that was stained with red, its bristles frozen into stiff peaks.

It was always cold on Trallit. Every time he'd been there it had been cold, but it had never once snowed. It sometimes rained the coldest, bitterest rain he had ever felt on any world: but it never, ever, snowed on Trallit. One of the quirks of the meteorology of this strange dimension.

It had taken him a week to discover that, despite snowfall and other strange changes, he was in fact on the third planet from with sun in the Sol system: that this was this dimension's Earth, despite all outward signs. The constellations were what had tipped him off: they had been off at first, until he'd noticed the Southern Cross in the sky. Not only was he on an Earth-like planet, but on the Southern Hemisphere of it as well.

The Trallit people were terrestrial, that should have been a hint. They looked just like the humans of his home dimension Earth, save for the fact that their complexion — at least the group following him — was different. He reasoned that this was the result of different long-term migration affects that were a consequence of the lack of snow patterning.

None of that mattered now. What mattered now was that this particular culture of the Trallit people had invented lasers, and that those lasers were being fired at him with increasing intensity.

Tallis ducked behind a corner and took several pained, deep breaths of the cold air, trying to steady himself. The air was so chilled that it felt like it pierced his lungs. He held his watch up to his ear and then shook it desperately. He smacked it several times and the red LED came on again, slowly facing back from nothing. He smiled and almost laughed with joy, but held onto himself for fear that the encroaching patrolmen would hear.

He depressed the buttons on the watch's sides and it bleeped to life. He looked up across the way to the slot on the wall it was indicating towards, the smile leaving his face as he heard the patrols getting closer.

The slot on the wall beckoned him, and he swallowed. Taking one last deep, full-lunged breath he ran across the open walkway in full view of the Trallit patrolmen. They opened fire, their weapons strafing across the night sky in wide arcs that followed him. He swallowed and kept running, making a bee-line for the alley wall without pausing.

One of the shots caught his fur coat, and he felt it

evaporate clean off of his shoulders as though it were happening in slow motion. Full intensity. They had dialed their lasers up to full intensity, a level they would have had to have called and gotten clearance to attain. Tallis would have cursed at this change in the dynamic, had he not been so focused on getting the exact angle of his approach on the wall.

He hit the wall just as the Trallit patrols were turning to corner to see it, and they watched him disappear into nothing, as though the brick had no substance to it at all.

They followed him, but came up solid against it, and began feeling along the creases in the red stone, finding nothing they could pass through. After a moment they became convinced that one of their blasts had in fact struck him, and began to phone in their reports.

***

Tallis landed on the grassy knoll of the park from where the portal opened several feet in the air, the sudden change in orientation making his inner ear do a flip and disoriented him. It was also day here, and the sudden change to cloudless brightness and warmth was a sudden shock as well — like having cold water thrown into the hot bath you were enjoying, suddenly.

He scrambled into a nearby tree line out of sight and waited there, eyeing the gap in the world he'd fallen through, waiting to see if anything but a cold breeze would follow him. After a long moment when nothing did, he smiled and started to laugh with relief.

Wiping tears of joy from his eyes, he checked the readout on his watch again. It read back a phosphorous blue colour. He tapped it twice to get it to change, and when it did not he started to laugh even harder. He stood up out of the veil of trees and spread his arms wide in good humour, casting them skyward and feeling the warm glow upon his skin.

"Home," he said, with peace and joy. Tallis was back on Earth.

COMING SOON!
THE TELLURIAN TERRORIST
BY JD RYOT & AMANDA LABONTÉ!

Cassidy Cane slips between worlds, traveling to bizarre planets and alternate Earths to find extraordinary new technologies and artifacts that might better humanity!

Cassidy goes by many titles -- archeologist, anthropologist, adventurer -- but none more fitting than that given to her on some strange worlds: Slipstreamer.

On a visit to the planet Alluvian, she gains a new title, one which might haunt her for the rest of her life and change the trajectory of her dimensional journey forever: The Tellurian Terrorist. How does Cassidy earn such a title? Find out in this shocking final arc of Slipstreamers Season One!

Coauthored with international bestseller
Amanda Labonté! Not to be missed!

ACKNOWLEDGEMENTS

The authors would like to pay special thanks to the *Slipstreamers* committee at Engen Books, including Amanda Labonté, Matthew LeDrew, Ali House, Ellen Curtis, Erin Vance, and, Lauralana Dunne.

Without their tireless efforts, none of this would have been possible.

Special thanks to this episode's editor, AJ Ryan.

Paul Carberry would also like to thank his wife, for her constant support. Rick for sitting through the rough draft with me. And Dana, for always being a brave explorer of new worlds and taking me on your adventures.

Paul Carberry is a huge proponent of the horror genre and its place in literature. He has two children, daughter Dana and son Rick, with his wife Leah.

Paul has published four novels with Engen Books: the three book *Zombies on the Rock* series, and, *Carcharodon*, both of which are international bestsellers.

He has also had numerous short stories featured in publication in anthologies such as *From the Rock* and *Terror Nova*, including The Light of Cabot Tower, Into the Forest, and Halloween Mummers.

JD Ryot is the reclusive creator of the *Slipstreamers* series from Engen Books. JD is an avid fan of young adult literature and adventure serials. When asked if they had come to this world through a portal themselves, JD Ryot refused to answer. No record of their birth has ever been found... on this world.